THE DISTANCE BETWEEN US

A Story of International Love and Murder

Kyla-Maree Simcoke

ISBN-13: 978-0-692-05938-8
Library of Congress Control Number: 2018900783

Editing and proofreading: Andrew Doty, editwright.com
Book design: Nehmen-Kodner, n-kcreative.com
Author photo: Christina Ahlheim, Charisma Photography

Printed in the United States of America

Published by: The Distance Between Us LLC
Saint Louis, Missouri
First Edition

To my loving family,
Jon, Alex, & Jessie… you are my life.

To Erica, the most courageous person I know.

PROLOGUE

Letting out a relieved moan as his climax abated, he collapsed on top of her. Between choppy breaths, she said, irritated, "Get off me. You are crushing me. Oh my god, you are so heavy." In one fluid motion of his muscular body, he rolled off and landed on his back with a muted thud, causing the brass headboard to bang against the timber wall. "Oh bloody hell, it's hot in here," she groaned as she wiped at the sweat pooling between her breasts and trickling down the sides of her ribs. "Why do we always have to come to this shithole when you can afford to take me to Griffith and stay in one of those flash hotels?"

He placed his forearm over his eyes, wishing to himself that she would just shut up and stop her frigging whinging. For a great piece of arse, he wasn't sure it was worth it anymore. They had been having an affair for almost a year now. In the beginning it was exciting as hell. It was thrilling to sneak away and have the hottest sex he'd had in years. She was strikingly beautiful, with the darkest wavy charcoal hair set against her olive complexion. Her eyes were dark brown with specks of gold. He'd gotten turned on like a dog in heat when he had first met her at his kid's school fete. He had married into money and liked the privileges that it brought into his life. Being married to a plain wife for ten years and having two kids wasn't so bad. He always justified to himself: if his wife couldn't give it up except on special occasions like his birthday, then why in the hell not get a little action from women who were more than willing? A few years ago his wife had found out about his indiscretions, and he stopped for fear of her leaving him—and with her all of her daddy's money. For too long now he'd thought he had to end this. His wife was showing signs of suspicion. He was going to run for the county council seat next month, and if the news of infidelity got out, his political career would be over. And so would his marriage and access to her hefty bank account.

Her complaining shattered his thoughts. "I feel so disgusting. Why don't you put in a decent shower? The muddy brown water that trickles out of the showerhead makes me feel even dirtier than when I got in. How am I supposed to wash the scent of you off me with that disgusting river water?"

Sitting up abruptly, he grabbed for his trousers and growled, "Don't you ever give it a rest, woman? I can be at home and hear this shit."

"What's gotten into you?"

"Nothing! Get dressed, I need to get home."

"What's the hurry? You said your wife was visiting her parents on the station for the weekend."

"She may ring, and if I'm not home, she'll start getting suspicious again. In fact, I think she already is. I can't let her know about you. Maybe we should take a break for a while." He stood up and put on his trousers. As he zipped his fly, she bolted out of bed and stood toe-to-toe with him.

She crooned in her sensuous voice, "Now come on, Babe, I'm sorry I was complaining. The heat makes me feel so miserable, and I get a little whiney. Come on, why don't you come back to bed and I'll make it up to you?" She reached for his hands and brought them up to cup her large, round breasts.

For a split second all he wanted to do was put his lips on her big brown nipples, suck them into his mouth, and get lost in her again. Suddenly, he realized he had to get back on track or lose everything. He had come from a hardworking family that had never had enough. He had sworn to himself when he had left home that he would never worry about where his next meal came from. He had worked too hard at university and law school, receiving top marks and honors which landed him a job in the prestigious law firm of McArthur and James. Marrying the boss's daughter was his reward for years of hard work. He wasn't about to blow it now.

Snapping his arms backward, he stepped back and freed his hands from her grip. He grabbed his wrinkled shirt, tie, and shoes and headed out of the bedroom, smelling of sweat and sex. Without turning back he growled, "Get dressed."

The woman gathered her clothes strewn all over the room and quickly got dressed, swearing under her breath with each article of clothing she put on. Stalking to the cabin door and slamming it on its hinges, she spat out, "I don't know what friggin' bug crawled up your arse tonight. I thought we had a good time in there. Just like you like it, hard and fast."

"Look, Blackie," he replied wearily. He wasn't in the mood to keep listening to her. "We have to call this off for a while. She knows something is going on. I can't get caught again. She meant it the last time when she said she would screw my balls to the wall."

"Oh come on, don't be a dumb prick. You were going to leave her anyway, right after the election. Once you win that you'll be set," she yelled.

"No, Blackie, I won't. Her dad has a lot of clout around here. I'd be kicked out on my sorry, cheating bum. I'd lose my job and reputation if her dad and his cronies found out I've committed adultery. I'd never be able to find a job around here, and I'd lose every penny I've earned," he shouted as he stalked down the stairs.

She flew down the stairs, grabbing him by the arm and flinging him around to face her. Her eyes had turned black, her anger searing into him. He caught his breath for a moment as a tingle of fear spiraled through him. She screamed wildly at him, "You are not tossing me into the dirt like a dried-up piece of kangaroo shit. I've given you the best fucks you'll ever have in your life. You're my ticket out of this shithole of a town," as she hammered her small fists against his broad chest.

He reached for her wrists and pulled her against him. In a low, menacing voice he hissed, "Cut this shit out. You knew I was never going to leave her. This was just about sex, nothing else. There was never going to be a future with you. Hear me? I was never going to leave her for you. You may be the best fuck in town, but that's all you are." He spat those final words into her face. He gave her a brutal shove. She was sent flying backward toward the cabin's railing, striking her head against a wooden column. Her back sheared against the wood as she sank to the ground.

She was momentarily dazed. Swearing as she got up on her knees, she felt something hard and painful dig into her leg, causing her to cry out. She reached down by her right leg and felt the solid wooden handle of an axe. He had already turned toward his car, yelling out, "It's over. Don't you ever try and bloody ring me or I'll make you wish you had never set eyes on me."

His threat slammed into her like a slap in the face. Insurmountable anger coursed through her as she jumped up and ran toward his retreating back. Flinging her arms back, she grasped the handle of the axe. She ran a few feet and thrust her arms downward, her rage propelling her forward. She struck him on the crown of his head and heard the loud echo of crushing bone as the axe pierced his skull.

PART 1

CHAPTER 1

Olivia Clark was at work at the Newsagent, her very first job at sixteen. Standing at the till ringing up Mr. Jessup's purchase of *The Riverine Grazier*, a pack of Winfield Blues, and a lotto ticket, she could hear the engine of a small plane. She wondered if it was her mum and dad flying back from Griffith. Since her father obtained his pilot's license, he'd been flying to Griffith in his Cessna a few times a month. Interrupting her thoughts, Mr. Jessup asked, "How's that old bugger of a grandfather doing? Heard he was crook last week."

"Much better, thanks. He caught that stomach bug that was going around. He got over it pretty quick. Nothing can keep him down."

"Yeah, tough old dog he is."

As she handed him his change, the building rocked with a loud explosion. The resounding deep, hollow, echoing sound of something blown up caused her to lose her balance and fall against the counter, dropping the coins. Holding onto the till, she righted herself and ran through the store and out the door, stopping abruptly on the footpath. Her heart was racing and her breathing ragged as she looked to the sky. Her gut wrenched. There was a cloud of black, billowing smoke in the direction of the bridge into South Hay. She ran into the street and stood in shock. There were dozens of people out in the street staring at the dark cloud of smoke. Cars stopped in the road, people yelling in shock. Olivia could hear people yelling, "What the bloody hell blew up? Did anyone see what happened?" She could hear the shrieking of a fire truck. Someone grabbed her arm and pulled her out of the middle of the road. "Come on, girl, get outta the way," she heard the man say as a fire truck, ambulance, and cop car came whizzing by. She pulled her arm free from the man's grip and took off in a sprint. She ran wildly toward the bridge, running around people, pushing her way through groups gawking at the site. She kept running as tears of fear gushed from her eyes, blinding her vision.

Her eyes flew open. The dark room disoriented her, her body trembling and her breathing rapid. Bolting upright in the bed, she wiped the tears from her cheeks. Her eyes instantly refocused on the familiar outlines of her furniture. Exhaling, she realized she was in her own bed and was reliving the memories of her parents' deaths. Slowing her breathing, she glanced at the alarm clock. Not quite 5:30 a.m. *I may as well get up*, Olivia thought to herself. There was no time for trying to go back to sleep—it was time to get ready for work.

Flipping on the light to the bathroom, she caught a glimpse of her wild strawberry blonde hair tangled in all directions. She remembered her mother brushing the tangles when she was little, always mumbling about what a rat's nest she had in the mornings. Olivia thought to the time her parents had died and how devastatingly hard it had been for her. If it hadn't been for her grandparents she couldn't be sure what direction her life would have taken. She was thankful for them, as she thought life had turned out pretty good, considering the circumstances. She was able to go to uni after she finished high school. She had attended the University of Sydney, where she earned her degree in nursing. Shortly after graduating, she obtained a job at the Royal Sydney Hospital until her grandfather passed away. She returned to her hometown of Hay, New South Wales to live with her widowed grandmother. She worked at the local bush hospital in the intensive care unit for a few years until her grandmother too passed away. Feeling the weight of loneliness consume her, she decided to move to the United States. She ran from the memories and complete emptiness she felt deep in her bones. The first time she had had these feelings was when her best mate Kev had left without warning. She had pushed her memories of him to the far recesses of her heart. If she allowed them to surface she would be overwhelmed with memories of all the people she had lost in her life, and they would certainly crush her. That's why she fled her home and country to start fresh in a place that held no memories. She was thankful she still had her favorite cousin Kerri. They talked frequently; Kerri was always bugging her about when she would be coming home. She wasn't ready just yet.

Forcing herself to return to the present, she set about getting herself ready for work. She dressed hurriedly, clipping her now untangled, wavy hair into a knot at the nape of her neck. Dressed in pressed dark slacks, a light turquoise blouse, black low-heeled shoes, and white starched lab jacket, she headed out the door. Olivia reversed into the quiet street in her blue sedan and began the ten-minute drive to the hospital. The sun had already begun to rise, showering the sky in a brilliant, pale pink that pushed the darkness of night away. She drove along the winding road that circumvented the lake and occasionally took her eyes off the road to peer at it. She loved the water and was always amazed how different it looked each day depending on the weather and where the sun was in the sky. So completely different in contrast to the muddy brown water of the Murrumbidgee River that she grew up beside.

A creature of habit, she parked her car at the very back of the parking lot, the same spot every day. Every morning she allowed herself a few minutes to step out of her car and stand to look at the lake. Each season it would take on a different look, depending on where the sun was in the sky. On a calm, cool morning like this, the sun barely peeking over the horizon, the light was reflected off the water in a slow, sultry way. Later in the day, the sun would be fully alert, casting brilliant, sharp light over the water, making it twinkle like dancing stars. In the winter, with deep, dark, menacing grey clouds and strong winds, the lake would appear to be in turmoil. Large waves with white caps slamming against each other, trying desperately to remain and not be taken by the wind.

Inhaling deeply, she turned and walked to the east entrance of the hospital. Harbor Lake Hospital was a small, country hospital with only sixty beds and a small emergency room that served the outlying rural communities. It was built in the '40s, a few years after the town had sprung up around the thirty-six-mile natural lake. People who wanted to live in a beautiful, quiet setting to raise their families had fled the bustle and chaos of St. Louis. As commerce flourished over the years, the town of Harbor Lake grew to a population of more than 30,000 people. The rural areas farther west had vastly grown as well, presenting the town with the need for a hospital. The closest hospital for Harbor Lake had been fifty miles away and even farther for the rural areas. The city leaders were able to raise the funds from private interests, assembled a board of directors, and broke ground March 23,

1943. Harbor Lake Hospital opened the doors to a very grateful community two years later on January 20, 1945.

Entering the sliding glass doors, she began thinking about her agenda for the day. Recalling she had a meeting with the daughters of Mrs. Parson, an eighty-seven-year-old woman who was suffering from end-stage lung cancer. She had coded twice, going into PEA each time. The pulseless electrical activity was caused by constant hypoxia. There was not enough oxygen in her blood to perfuse her organs. Her lungs were finished; she had been on a ventilator for nine days and was declining more each day. Her two older daughters wanted to respect their mother's wishes and allow her to pass. The youngest daughter was fighting them every step of the way. She was so buried in her denial she would not accept that her mother was dying.

After stopping briefly in her office to lock up her purse and print off the list of consults for the day, Olivia walked into the intensive care unit and immediately followed the scent of freshly-brewed coffee. Walking over to the kitchen station, Olivia was greeted by her long-time coworkers and friends Hazel, Ronnie, and Jay. Hazel, barely reaching 5' 1", had short blonde hair with sprinkles of grey, and the kindest pale blue eyes. She had been a nurse for thirty years. Ronnie was the opposite of Hazel—standing at 5' 9", skinny as a rail with bright red hair in a tangle of curls that she wore in a ponytail high on her head. She had been a nurse for ten years and had youthful energy. Her mouth had no filter, saying whatever came to mind. Jay was the only male nurse in the unit and was adored by everyone. Having been a nurse for fifteen years, he brought with him an arsenal of knowledge and skill. He was 5' 6" with short, dark hair that was spiked on top and held in place with gel. He was the resident adrenaline junky who relished in the critical patient who was crashing. He would be in his element flying around the room participating in procedures and life-saving protocols.

"Morning, Olivia," they said in unison with sleepy smiles on their faces.

"Morning. Looks like your first cup hasn't kicked in. You all look tired."

Ronnie groaned, "Ah, Olivia, we didn't get out of here until after nine last night. Right at the end of shift change we got a GI bleed with a hemoglobin of four."

"It was hit-the-doors-running when he got up here from the ER. Both day- and night shifts pulled together and got him stabilized pretty quickly. We still didn't get out 'til late," Hazel said as she stifled a yawn.

Jay, turning with coffee pot in hand, began to fill Olivia's cup. "You're gonna need this. You're in for a rough day with Mrs. Parson's daughters. They were at each other pretty bad last night, all three of them leaving in tears."

Olivia closed her eyes briefly and sighed, "It's so sad. This case has been very difficult. I'm not sure what else I can do. It's a stalemate."

"Come on; it's a no-brainer, no pun intended. It doesn't take a rocket scientist to see her mother's brain is already toast," Ronnie exclaimed.

"Oh, come now, Ronnie, her daughter just doesn't understand," Hazel said, "We have to give her some time."

"How much time? When her mother starts to rot like a corpse?" Ronnie replied.

"Come on, guys, I know it's tough on you too," said Olivia.

"Tough on us! I'll tell you what's tough. It's taking care of a person who is already dead. She's not there. I look at the damn numbers beeping across the monitor and know if we took everything off her, they would stop," Ronnie said, close to tears.

"I know it's awful and it's hard, but we have to keep caring for her just like we would if we knew she would recover. She will be able to die, it's taking a little longer than nature intended," explained Olivia.

"I know, I know, it just makes me so sad for her. No one should have to suffer in death. I guess I've been doing this too long. It never gets easier," Ronnie sighed.

Jay placed a hand on Ronnie's shoulder, "Come on, let's go care for the ones we can help go home." They both walked off discussing what they needed to do in room five.

Hazel sadly watched them go. Turning to Olivia, she explained, "Ronnie doesn't mean to be so angry, it's just so hard. It makes us feel like we are doing the wrong thing. You know how 'we do no harm'? Well, it feels like we are. I know Mrs. Parson wrote an advance directive. She didn't want any of this. And here we are doing everything she said not to do. How can that be right, Olivia?"

Olivia was about to answer when Hazel said, "We aren't following her wishes," the frustration clear in her voice.

Olivia nodded her head, "I know. We run in to this when families don't understand or can't let go of a loved one. The confusing thing is that the advance directive is a legal document intended to tell us the patient's wishes if there is no hope for recovery. It should be upheld by the physician, but you know as well as I do this doesn't happen when there is family disputing it. It puts the physician in the middle of a very bad dilemma. He wants to do the right thing and follow the patient's wishes but is torn when the family are going against it. His hands are tied. If he follows the AD then it could open him up to legal issues or worse. There's no winning in situations like these."

"I don't get it, Olivia, how can they just disregard a person's wishes?"

"It's frustrating and confusing. The whole intention of the patient writing out their wishes while they are competent is so when they can't tell us anymore, the AD is to be their voice."

"Well, if it's their voice, why isn't anyone listening?"

"Because some people can't deal with the reality of letting their loved one go. I think medical technology has come so far, it has now blurred the boundaries of life and death. People think we can save everyone and help them live forever." Taking Hazel's hand, Olivia reassuringly said, "We will do the right thing for Mrs. Parson. I'm trying to let her voice be heard. I have another ethics meeting with the daughters at ten this morning. I'll let you know how it goes."

"Good luck, you're going to need it."

CHAPTER 2

Olivia felt weary as she walked out the hospital's back entrance at the end of the day. Thinking of the meeting she'd had with the Parson sisters, she felt incredibly sad and disappointed. Dr. David O'Day, Palliative Care director; Dr. Leonard, an ICU physician; Sister Beatrice; and herself had failed yet again to convince the youngest sister, Lillian, that her mother was never going to recover.

The meeting ended abruptly when Lillian screamed at the group that they were murderers. She had fled the room distraught. The two older sisters, Ruby and Ida, had apologized, embarrassed with their sister's outburst. Olivia reached her car, stopped, and stared over the lake. The water was calm, which brought her a sense of peace. She felt some tension fall away when she heard a timid voice, "Olivia." She turned to see Lillian Parson standing before her. She looked older than she had weeks ago. Now she looked defeated and older than her sixty years. Her dress was hanging off her thin frame, her eyes were puffy and her face deeply lined in sagging wrinkles. Her eyes held a deep sadness that made Olivia want to hug her and take her pain away.

"Oh, Lillian," Olivia replied.

"I'm sorry for what I said today, especially for screaming at all of you," her voice held true regret. Olivia stepped closer to her and reached for her hand, "I understand, I know how you feel."

Lillian pulled her hand free. "How could you possibly know what I'm going through?"

"I lost my parents too," Olivia replied sadly.

Startled, Lillian looked into her eyes and was briefly speechless. "I'm so sorry, Olivia, I had no idea. I assumed since you were so young—" Turning, she covered her eyes, "Oh my gosh. I've been so caught up in the fact that mother's not going to be here with me anymore, I'm drowning in this pain. I've given no consideration to anyone else. My poor sisters, oh my goodness. I've been so hateful to them. How will they ever forgive me?"

"Lillian, they have already forgiven you. They understand how hard it has been on all of you, especially you." Cautiously Olivia stated, "This is the first time I have heard you acknowledge that your mother is not going to be with you anymore."

Sighing in defeat, Lillian explained, "I guess in my mind I have always known, but I refused to allow my heart to acknowledge it. If I admitted to myself, then her dying would be real. Keeping her here at the hospital allowed me to believe she was still with me. I can't imagine living in a world without my mother." Wiping the tears that were falling onto her cheeks, she continued, "My mother has been the one true person who has always been there for me, being so much younger than my sisters and raised without a father. He left when I was born; I never knew him. I blamed myself that he left. He didn't want another child. So Mother gave me the love of two parents and always made me feel wanted." Looking at Olivia, she questioned, "With Mother gone, who's going to be there for me?"

The crushing feeling of being left alone jolted through Olivia. She had felt the exact same helplessness and loneliness after Kev disappeared, then after her parents and grandparents had died. Pushing these feelings away, she said, "Lillian, you have forgotten you have family who love you too: your husband and your sisters. You are not alone."

Nodding, Lillian mumbled, "I'm going to go back and sit with her for a while." She turned and walked away. Olivia watched her walk away, stared at her retreating back. Thinking to herself, *That was me*.

CHAPTER 3

After an exhausting day, Olivia had gone to bed early. She was in a deep sleep, dreaming of her childhood. Waking to the sound of meowing coming from the neighbors' old tabby Matilda reminded Olivia briefly that she should have closed the window last night. She couldn't have, as she would've tossed and turned all night in the summer heat. This Christmas season was one of the hottest summers on record. With no central air conditioning, Olivia had to rely on her fan, an occasional breeze through the window, and the water cooler, which was sputtering and gurgling because it was almost out of water. Rolling over and placing a pillow over her head, she tried to drown out the morning noises and go back to sleep. Then she suddenly remembered. Rolling onto her back and kicking off the sheet, she muttered to herself, "Oh bugger, I'm supposed to meet Kev." The night before, Kev had rung and they had made plans to meet across the street from her house and ride down to the river on their bikes. Kev was to bring the meat that had gone off, the string, a net, and a bucket for yabby fishing. Her grandmother especially liked a good yabby boil. She called them the prawns of the river.

She quickly got up and changed into shorts, a T-shirt, and a pair of sand shoes. She quietly tiptoed to the toilet, avoiding certain floorboards for the loud creak they would make. She didn't want to wake her mum and dad up, as they were up late 'til the pub closed. Saturday nights at the pub were often busy and the locals got a bit rowdy. She glanced at her watch; it was only 7:00 a.m. She had time to make a few pieces of toast with vegemite. She wasn't meeting Kev until 7:30 a.m. The kitchen was at the back of the house, away from her parents' room, so she didn't need to be so quiet. Taking the matches down from the shelf, she lit the gas burner, then placed the mesh wire toaster over the flame. Taking two slices of bread from the tin breadbox, she placed them both on the toaster. She kept the flame low so she wouldn't burn the bread and have to scrape the black off the toast with a knife, as she did at Grandmother's house. Grandmother had a habit of burning the toast 'til it was black like charcoal.

Flipping the toast to brown the other side, she walked over to the cupboard, lifting the latch upward, then to the side. The kitchen floor was dipped downward, causing the cupboard to lean sideways. It was an old house, and all the floors were a little uneven and creaky. Olivia didn't mind the woodwork and older style of the home; they lent character to it. At least, that's what her dad said when her mum got upset that things were falling apart. Finishing her breakfast, she placed the dishes in the sink, left by the back door, and got onto her bike. She headed out into the lane, turned left down Hatty St. toward the river road.

Braking beside the dirt road, Olivia looked around for Kev. *That's weird*, she thought, *Kev's never late*. Getting off her bike and pushing the kickstand down with her shoe, she sat down under a tree and waited. She picked up a small stick and began doodling in the dirt, not paying attention to what she was drawing. Lost in thought, she was suddenly startled as an old, rusted Ute came slowly down the road. She looked up to see Jacko Flinders with a smoke hanging out his mouth and his worn Akubra slung low on his head, so you could barely see his bloodshot eyes. He braked slowly, coming to a rolling stop, and leaned out of the window.

"G'day, 'ow ya goin'? You and Kev goin' yabby fishin' this morning?"

"Mornin', Jacko, yeah, I'm just waiting on Kev to show up. He should be here in a few." He took the cigarette from his mouth, exhaling a bloom of smoke and flicking the butt into the ashtray. He said in his low gravelly voice from years of two packs per day, "He better make a move on, it's gonna be bloody hotter than a witch's tit by lunchtime. Tipping his fingers off his bushy grey eyebrows and accelerating, he called out, "Hooroo."

Olivia returned to her doodling, then stopped and stared at what she had actually drawn in the dirt: several hearts of all sizes with the letters "KA & OC." She stared at the initials and quickly erased them with her hand, looking around embarrassedly. Shaking her head to clear it, she thought, *Mum said I'd start liking boys in different ways now that I'm almost thirteen. But Kev? How silly is that? Kev's my best mate*. Jumping up and pushing away those crazy thoughts, she brushed the dirt off her bum and got on her bike. Looking at her watch, she saw it was after 7:30 a.m. *Kev should have been here by now*, she thought. She wondered if he overslept or his mum wouldn't let him go.

She started peddling down Water St., turned left on Pine St., then right on to Moppett St. Stopping at the crosswalk on Lachlan St., which was the Cobb Highway, she waited for a few cars to pass, then ducked across the street by the newsagents and turned down McGregor St.

Arriving at the one-story house with the sloping verandah, she jumped off her bike and walked up to the front door. She was about to knock on the screen door, then thought if his parents were sleeping she didn't want to wake them up. She walked back down the verandah steps, taking a right to the side of the house. She stepped on some crumbling bricks and peered into Kev's bedroom window. The blind was up and the curtains were slightly parted in the middle, so she could see into the room. The bed was made, and the room looked empty of Kev's stuff. Confused, she stumbled off the bricks and stood looking at the empty house. She ran to the front yard, jumped on her bike, and turned left into the alley. She pedaled to the back of the house, finding there were no cars there. *That's really weird*, she thought, *where would they be this early on a Sunday morning? Why didn't Kev tell me they were going on a trip? Or maybe Jimmy's mum got sick during the night and they had to take off to Narrandera?* Disappointed, she went back the way she came and slowly pedaled home.

Arriving home, she entered the back door, noticing it was still quiet. Her parents must have still been sleeping. Thinking of what to do with herself today, she decided she may as well catch up on her reading. Being on school holidays over Christmas had not left much time for her favorite pastime. Getting the bucket, she went into the bathroom and filled it up with cold water from the bathtub. Carefully filling the water cooler, adjusting the control to high and positioning it toward her bed, she stepped out of her sandshoes, picked up the latest Nancy Drew book, and lay down to read.

In her dream, she could hear her mother's voice gently calling her name and felt like she was been tousled. Slowly waking, she realized her mum was really calling her name and gently rocking her shoulders. "Come on, Liv, wakie, wakie, time to get up, sleepyhead." Rolling over and smiling sleepily up at her mum, she whispered, "What time is it? I don't have school today, do I?"

Laughing, her mum said, "No, silly, it's two o'clock in the afternoon. You fell asleep while reading. Dad and I didn't want to wake you up, so we let you get your beauty rest."

Olivia placed her arm over her forehead. "Oh, mum, I slept the day away," she said disappointedly. "Well, it doesn't matter; I didn't have anything to do today anyway. Suddenly becoming wide awake and slightly anxious, Olivia sat up and said, "Mum, Kev was s'posed to meet me at the river road, we were gonna go yabby fishin' and he didn't show up. So I rode to his house and no one was home. Jimmy and Victoria's cars were gone. Kev's bedroom looked empty of all his stuff." She felt a rising panic as she recalled the events of the morning.

Placing her hands on Olivia's shoulders, her mother firmly said, "Now, calm down, you are getting yourself all worked up. I'm sure everything is alright. They probably had to take off quickly if Jimmy's mum became sick. I'm sure he'll ring you later tonight. Now come on and get ready, we are leaving for the pub in a half an hour. Grandmother's Sunday roast will be ready shortly, and I've got to get there and make the gravy." Her mouth started to water and her tummy gave a low rumble as she realized she was starving—all she had eaten today were two pieces of toast for brekkie. After changing into a sundress and sandals, Olivia finished brushing her strawberry, honey-blonde hair. She pulled her hair back and secured it on top of her head with an oyster shell comb her mum had given her for Christmas. Her hair hung loosely in soft waves down her back. Looking in the mirror, she was surprised to notice she didn't feel so awkward in a dress. She kinda looked nice, like a girl. For years her family has teased her that she ran around like a tomboy. Her mum and grandmother always pleaded with her to wear a dress and act more like a young lady. She told them it was not very practical to wear a dress and nice sandals to go fishing, climb trees, or ride her bike. She conceded on Sundays for roast dinners she would wear a dress and act like a girl. Twirling in the mirror once, she thought wearing a dress wasn't so bad.

Pulling up beside her grandparents' dark purple Mercedes Benz, Olivia and her parents, Mick and Sarah, got out of the Ford Fairlane and walked up the gravel driveway to the back staircase that led to the kitchen. Her parents were behind, holding hands, while Olivia skipped up the steps, calling back, "Come on, you two, hurry up. I'm starving." Opening the green, wooden screen door, Olivia rushed into the kitchen and stopped as she stood and inhaled the delicious aromas of roast lamb, roasted veggies, and fresh, homemade scones just out of the oven. Her mouth watering, she rushed over to her grandmother standing at the kitchen counter mixing something in a bowl. Wrapping her arms around her grandmother's waist, Olivia said lovingly, "Hello, Grandmother, oh it smells so beautiful, is it ready? I'm so hungry."

Returning the hug and giving Olivia a quick kiss on her cheek, she said, "As soon as your mum makes the gravy and your dad carves the leg of lamb, we will be ready to eat. Now, why don't you go set the table in the ballroom."

"Alright," Olivia said joyfully as she ran to the swinging door into the galley. Getting five settings of cutlery, water glasses, and serviettes down from the cupboards, she placed them all carefully on the silver trolley. She pushed it through the door to the ballroom, by the smaller round table near the French doors, so they would feel the late afternoon breeze as they ate. Normally she would have set the table for eight, but since Kev and his parents weren't there she set it for five.

Olivia walked back into the kitchen as Grandfather came in the back door. He looked stern as always, dressed in pressed slacks and a white button shirt and his thick white and silver hair combed neatly in place, oddly contrasting with his ruddy red face. At 6' 2" with a round beer belly, he always dressed professionally as the publican. Olivia didn't recall him ever dressing in anything but his dress clothes. She didn't even think he owned a pair of tennis shoes.

"Hello, Grandfather," Olivia called out.

Replying gruffly, he said, "G'day, have you set the table?"

"Yes, it's already set."

Grandmother was serving up the carved lamb, roasted potatoes, pumpkin, onions, and peas. Sarah finished pouring the gravy into a bowl and asked Olivia to get the gravy ladle. With the food dished up, everyone picked up their plates and went to sit down at the table.

Mick asked Sarah and his parents what they wanted to drink as he headed over to the bar in the back of the room. All the adults asked for a cold stubby of beer, and Olivia asked for a lemonade.

The roast was amazing, Olivia thought as she savored the juicy lamb with mint sauce. She loved her mum's and grandmother's roast dinners, something to look forward to on Sundays. Conversation was general about the pub, who came in on Saturday night and what needed to be ordered on Monday. Several times, Olivia tried to tell her grandmother about Kev not being home this morning, but her grandfather would interrupt and change the subject. She was not allowed to interrupt when her grandfather was speaking, so she kept quiet and continued eating, miffed as to why her grandfather kept cutting her off.

Once everyone had finished eating, Grandmother turned to Olivia and said, "Come on, love, why don't you help me clear the dishes." Olivia gathered the dishes and took them into the kitchen. Her mother started washing while Grandmother started putting the food away. Sarah asked her to go in and make sure the table was cleared off. She went to the table and began picking up the serviettes and salt and pepper shakers when she overheard Jimmy's name mentioned. She crept over to the doorway and stood silently beside the doorframe. She heard her father and grandfather speaking quietly with concern in their voices. They were both standing with their backs toward her by the verandah railing, so she really had to strain to hear what they were saying. She turned her head closer to the doorway, trying hard to conceal herself.

She heard her father say, "Struth, what a bloody mess."

"She really stuck it to him good. How are we gonna get him out of this mess."

"She framed him pretty good. Now she's taken off with Kev."

Olivia couldn't hear the rest of what her father was saying as a semi-trailer came rumbling loudly past the front of the pub. As the noise trailed off she heard her grandfather say, "We won't see her again. I guarantee she's disappeared for good."

Olivia stifled a cry and stepped through the doorway with a look of pure shock on her face. She stood there, immobile, while staring at her father. "Dad," she choked out, "Kev?"

Grandfather raised his voice, "What are you doing there and—"

Mick quickly cut him off, "Dad, give me a tick." Taking his daughter in his arms, he spoke softly into her hair. "Now, love, there's a lot you won't understand, and I'll try and explain as best I can. Kev's mum has done something very bad and blamed it on Jimmy. She has run off with Kev. There are people out there looking for her."

"Will they find her? Will Kev come back?"

"I dunno, love."

Pulling back from her father with tears streaming down her face, she screamed "No!" Not wanting to believe the truth written on her dad's face, she turned and ran. She chanted "no" over and over as she ran through the galley and slammed the door against the wall. She ran the length of the kitchen, flying out of the screen door and leaving it shuddering on its hinges.

Grandmother and Sarah looked bewildered as the kitchen screen door swung back, hitting the door frame with a loud bang. They both called out her name in surprise. As Sarah threw down the dishcloth to go after her, Mick ran in through the galley doors. Reaching for Sarah, he anxiously said, "Hold on, Lovie."

"What, Mick? What's going on?" she asked with fear in her eyes. Placing both hands over his face and letting out a frustrated sigh, he turned to his wife and mother and explained what little he knew. Both women were stunned; they couldn't imagine a murder, things like that didn't happen around here. It couldn't be possible. "Where did they go? Will they ever be back?" Sarah asked. Feeling an enormous sense of dread, he said, "I dunno. If she really killed that bloke then she's gone for good. She set up Jimmy, she won't be back."

"Oh, no," Sarah said as she began to cry.

Looking up at her husband, unable to stop her tears, Sarah said, "I have to go and find Olivia; she's going to be devastated. Where could she have gone?"

Pain crinkling his face, Mick said, "Oh, bloody hell."

Placing a hand on Sarah's arm, Grandmother said with fierceness in her eyes, "Let me go, dear, I'll talk to Olivia. I know where she'll be." Feeling relieved, Sarah nodded. She knew by the look on her mother-in-law's face that she was ready to do battle. For such a tiny woman, she was a force to reckon with if her family was hurt. She would find Olivia and help ease her pain.

Olivia was silently sobbing as she sat wedged in front of the unused fireplace and behind the couch. This had been her secret hiding place since she was little. When her grandfather yelled at her, she would run up to the upstairs foyer outside of the ballroom and hide behind the couch. She was unaware that her grandmother had sat down on the couch until she heard her softly say "Livie." Holding her face in her hands, leaning onto her bent knees, Olivia continued to sob. "Liv, I know you are terribly sad and can't believe what's happened. It's alright to cry. Why don't you come out and sit with me," Grandmother said soothingly. Not moving, Olivia continued to cry.

"Come on, love, come sit with me, and we will have a chat." Slowly Olivia straightened up and pulled herself up by holding onto the back of the couch. On wobbly legs, she walked around the couch and fell into her grandmother's arms. Stroking her hair and holding her tightly in her arms,

Grandmother gently planted kisses on her forehead, rocked her back and forth, and repeated, "It's going to be alright, it's alright."

Several minutes later Olivia disengaged herself from her grandmother, sitting up on her knees and looking into her softly wrinkled face. "Oh, how can this be alright? I'll never be okay without Kev. We have been mates since we were little. I've spent almost every day of my life with him and shared every thought and experience. He is a part of me. Why did this happen? Why did he have to leave? I don't understand!" she cried out as she started choking on fresh tears. Grandmother handed her a hanky to wipe her nose and soak up the falling tears. "Grandmother, it hurts so badly, I feel my chest is going to explode and I can't breathe,"

"Now, come here and lay your head on my lap."

She did as she was told. Her breathing began to ease, her sobbing slowed and became regular as Grandmother stroked her back and her face. She listened as Grandmother explained. "Liv, life is not easy and it's not always fair. We learn to cope with what comes our way and try our best to get through it. Having those you hold dear to you makes it easier, but losing them makes the next step harder, but not impossible. You and Kev shared a very special bond that not many people experience in a lifetime. You have been very lucky. Kev has to go away for now. You two were meant to be together and you will find your way back to each other one day."

Sitting up, Olivia asked, "How can you know? He is gone and I don't know where he went."

Holding her face in her soft, wrinkled hands and looking intently into her eyes, Grandmother whispered with conviction, “You will be together again, believe me. You will be together.”

Olivia woke up suddenly and reached for her face to wipe away the tears, realizing she was dreaming again of Kev. He had followed her in her dreams for years. The talk with Mrs. Parson yesterday had brought all those years of missing him back. He has got to be alive somewhere, but where? “Grandmother, you said we’d be together some day. I don’t believe you anymore!” she cried out loud and rolled over and put a pillow over her head.

CHAPTER 4

Having just finished her report, Suzanna took the last sip of her morning coffee and gathered her papers and stethoscope. She was ready to start her morning assessments of her patients, and knowing she needed help turning the patient in Room 7, she called out, "Hey, Blair, can you help me with a turn in Room 7?"

"Sure, I'll be right there," Suzanna replied as she, too, was taking the last sip of her coffee. Suzanna met Blair in Room 7, and Suzanna looked at the patient, who appeared to be sedated and breathing well with the assistance of the ventilator. "So what's this guy's story?"

Suzanna, who was assessing the patient's neuro status, looked up. "Oh, poor guy has been battling chronic lymphocytic leukemia since his twenties. He did really well staying in remission for several years. About two weeks ago he became sick again. His white count is down and now he is septic. He is having a hard time getting through it. We have him on all the big-gun antibiotics, which are knocking his kidneys around. His creatinine was elevated, went into respiratory failure secondary to developing pneumonia, probably from being on the vent so long, and we are having trouble keeping his pressure up. Have him on Levophed, which I'm trying to wean him off."

"Doesn't sound good. He looks so young and healthy to be so sick," Blair observed as she began rearranging the multitude of wires and tubing so they could turn him on his side. Stopping to look at the patient's face, Suzanna sadly replied, "Yeah, he does. He was really active and worked out a lot. He often did the 5Ks and even did the triathlon here at the lake last year. I've taken care of him the past two times he had a relapse. He is a really nice guy with a great sense of humor."

They both prepared to turn him, first adjusting the vent tubing so as not to accidently extubate him. Each on either side of the bed, they gathered their two corners of the pad, counted to three, and pulled him up and over to the right of the bed so they could turn him on his side. Suzanna took her stethoscope from her ears after assessing his lung sounds. She reached for the lotion and massaged some on his back, all the while assessing his skin for any breakdown. Blair held onto his shoulder and hip to keep him on his side. She asked, "Does he have any family?"

"Yeah, he only has his mom, he's not married. Surprising for such a good-looking man. He told me once that he didn't want to go through this again if things didn't look good. He wanted everything stopped."

Perplexed, Blair asked, "Then why are we still doing this to him? How long has he been on the vent?

Sighing, Suzanna replied, "About a week. His mother is determined that he will recover. She said he has come out of this before and he will again."

"Does he have an advance directive?"

"Yes, it's in the chart."

With a hint of anger in her voice, Blair said, "Well, it may be written in invisible ink for all the good it does. It's not right, why do so many family members disregard their family's wishes?"

"'Cause they are scared of the unknown and what-ifs. They cling to the only thing they have left—hope. They feel like if they agree with the advance directive they are killing them," Suzanna tried to explain.

"I know, I know, I've heard it all before. Wish people would get educated and realize in some instances all this medical intervention just prolongs their death and causes horrible suffering," Blair said.

Propping pillows behind his back and one between his knees to keep him positioned on his side, they covered him with a sheet. As Suzanna began suctioning his endotracheal tube, Blair pulled off gloves and threw them in the trash harder than was necessary. As she began washing her hands, she turned to Suzanna and said, "I'm putting in a palliative care consult, something needs to be done."

Startled, Suzanna looked at Blair and anxiously replied, "No, not yet, I still think he could make it out of this. He is young and strong."

"Oh, come on, he is already going into multi-organ failure. Get real."

Suzanna straightened up, placing both hands on the side rail, and angrily spat out, "Keep out of this, he is not your patient, and you know nothing about his prognosis." Dismissing her, she said firmly, "Thanks for the help. I've got it from here."

Blair turned and stormed out of the room after slinging back the curtain and almost ripping it off the track. She headed for the phone and dialed. After a few rings, she heard, "Palliative care, this is Olivia."

"This is Blair, I've got a consult for you."

Fishing into her lab jacket for a pen, Olivia asked, "Okay, what's the patient's name?"

Caught off guard, she hesitated, then answered, "Ah, I don't know. He's in ICU 7."

"Is he your patient?" Olivia asked, perplexed.

"Well, no, I just heard of his case, and his nurse Suzanna thinks he doesn't need a consult."

"Then why are you calling one in?"

Angrily, she replied, "Because he is dying and his mother won't follow his advance directive. Just like all the other selfish families out there."

"Now hold on a minute, this isn't even your patient, and I don't think you have all the information to make this decision. Have you talked to the physician?"

"No, I don't need to. I know enough to know when we are drawing out yet another death," she angrily muttered.

Sighing, Olivia replied, "I'll take a look at his medical record and talk to the ICU doc and go from there, okay?"

Sarcastically, Blair replied, "Oh, do what you want," and slammed the phone into the receiver. After hearing the loud slam of the phone ringing in her ear, Olivia placed her phone down and muttered, "Whoa, what was that all about?" Olivia had known Blair over the years to be a good critical care nurse, but lately everyone had noticed the signs of burnout creeping up in her. Too many years of taking care of critically ill patients who endure so many invasive interventions that only prolong the inevitable can take a toll on a nurse. *In today's medicine,* thought Olivia, *there are so many advances in medical technology, patients are subjected to various life-saving interventions with a high rate of success. The technology has come so far it has now blurred the boundaries of life and death. People are living longer, but at what cost? So many lose the quality of life and just exist, robbing them of the natural process of dying. It makes many question: Are we living life or just existing?* Shaking off the feeling of unease, Olivia went into the ICU and found Room 7's chart on the rack. She found an empty chair in the back area of the nurse's station and began to read.

Kevin Anderson. Age: 28. Diagnosis: sepsis secondary to chronic lymphocytic leukemia. Admitted October 3rd, 2004. She then noted his advance directive filed in the back of the chart. It held the usual medical jargon found in most advance directives. "Medical procedures that only serve to prolong the dying process be withheld or withdrawn if at some point he or she is comatose and has an incurable or irreversible medical condition which could generally only be prolonged by extraordinary measures." The directive clearly stated the patient's wishes and was legally signed, witnessed, and notarized. Olivia pondered all the information she had gathered. Now the most challenging question: Was the patient's condition incurable or irreversible? This she needed to have answered. From experience Olivia knew the answer could easily be found in some cases. A patient who had severe hypoxic brain injury and had met criteria for clinically meeting brain death, was clearly in an irreversible condition. In other cases the waters could be very muddy and only time and continued treatment would provide the answer.

She placed the chart back in the chart rack and looked for Suzanna. They had first met several years ago when they started working together in the ICU and hit it off right away. Now they were each other's confidants and best friends. They were opposites in many ways but were able to find common ground. Suzanna, ten years older than Olivia, stood at only 5' tall. She had a tiny bone structure and curly blonde hair with an olive complexion that brought out the aqua in her big blue eyes. Suzanna, having grown up in the boondocks of Missouri, was a God-loving country girl. Olivia, having grown up in the bush of Australia, could connect with Suzanna on a genuine, sincere level. One of the things Olivia loved about Suzanna was her honesty. She would call Olivia out if she thought she was wrong and help her rethink. She found her in the clean utility room, gathering supplies for a patient's bed bath. Olivia smiled and said, "Hi, Suzanna, how are you?"

Returning the smile, she replied, "Oh fine, today is not too bad, actually got to take a break and pee."

"Yeah, I remember those days all too well, not getting a break. I don't miss those days at all. I was looking for you because I wanted to talk to you about Room 7."

"Oh, that bitch! Did she put in a consult to you? I can't believe it. She doesn't know anything about him and she takes it upon herself to call you? Sorry, but she is way out of line. Unbelievable. Who does she think she is? The angel of frigging mercy?"

Olivia held her hands up, "Whoa, hang on, it's okay. I know she over stepped her bounds and has jumped to conclusions without really knowing the situation. I'll have a talk with her. She is really burnt out."

Suzanna was seething, "I don't care. Maybe she should get out of here and try something different. Like the morgue."

"Let me look into this case, I'll talk with the doctors and meet with the mother and figure out where we are at. Don't worry; no one's doing anything at this point. Keep giving him all of your great care."

Her shoulders sagged as she felt relieved and said, "Thanks, I'm not giving up on him. He has a chance. He has beaten this before."

Olivia gave her a quick hug. "I'll keep you updated. I'm going to go speak with his mother."

Olivia left the utility room. As she passed the med room, Hazel walked out. "Hey, Olivia."

"Morning, how are you?"

"I need to tell you—"

"I'm in a rush, can we talk later?"

"Mrs. Parson passed away last night."

Stopping, Olivia asked in surprise, "What happened? Did Lillian finally agree to let her go?"

"No, she passed on her own. She coded again, and the three daughters told us to stop. They couldn't see her go through all of that again. To be honest, we weren't going to get her back. Her body just couldn't function anymore." Feeling a huge weight had been lifted, Olivia replied, "I'm glad Lillian didn't have to make the decision, it was taken out of her hands. She finally knew in her heart that this had to happen. I'm so relieved that she didn't have to voice the words."

Hazel agreed. "I think she'll be alright. When she left last night, her sisters were with her. It was strange—her face looked different, all the torment of the past weeks was gone."

Smiling, Olivia touched Hazel's shoulder, "Thanks for all your kindness you gave them. You are a good nurse." Blushing, Hazel said, "I thought you were in a rush; you better hurry up and go."

CHAPTER 5

Olivia walked briskly down the hallway, navigating around all the nurses rushing from room to room to attend to their patients' needs. The noise from the call lights, the constant dinging alarms from the monitors, and the endless ringing of the phones were normal noises on any busy floor. Olivia entered the deserted waiting room. She was about to turn to leave when she noticed an elegantly dressed woman sitting in the dark corner by the window. Olivia walked slowly toward her. She was beautiful. Olivia guessed she was in her late fifties, yet she still held remnants of beauty from youth. Her charcoal-colored hair was softly curled, barely reaching her shoulders. She had the most beautiful olive complexion with startling deep brown eyes. Reaching her, Olivia smiled and softly asked, "Are you Mr. Anderson's mother?"

Straining to smile, the woman replied, "Yes, I'm Victoria Price."

"It's nice to meet you. I'm Olivia Clark with Palliative Care."

Olivia thought she saw a flicker of surprise cross the woman's face, but as soon as it was there it was gone. Mrs. Price stood up abruptly and sternly stated, "We have nothing to talk about, Miss Clark. I am not interested in what you have to say. My son will not be taken off life support. I'd appreciate if you'd stay away from me and my son." With that she quickly walked out of the room. Olivia stood there, stunned. Never had she had a family member react so strongly in the introduction meeting.

The rest of the day went smoothly as she checked on other patients and met with their families to offer advice, information, or general support. The meeting with Mrs. Price was in the back of her mind all day. She couldn't shake how strangely the woman reacted. Something kept nagging at her and she couldn't quite put her finger on what it was. She had never met this woman before, but somehow she seemed familiar. From where, Olivia couldn't fathom.

At the end of the day she stopped by the unit to talk with longtime coworker and friend Dr. Edmonds. She found him at the back of nurse's station charting. "Hey, George," she said as she pulled up a chair beside him.

"Hi there, Olivia."

"I wanted to ask you about the patient in Room 7. I've reviewed his chart; it looks like the sepsis is pretty bad. I did notice his chest X-ray shows a slight improvement in the lower lobe infiltrates and his creatinine hasn't increased the past few days. Urine output has improved."

George responded, "He's still critical, though I'm seeing improvements every day. I think he has a good chance of recovering from this. If it weren't for his age and good physical fitness, I doubt he would recover. I'm optimistic."

"Hmm, that's good to hear."

"Why the sudden interest? He isn't someone that needs palliative care."

"I know. Blair called me about him, ranting that we weren't following his wishes."

"Oh no, she's at it again. She's been a great nurse over the years, but I think it's time for her to make a change."

"I like her passion and advocating for people, but she's going overboard in this case."

"Yes, she is. This guy will make it through this. I'll have a word with her."

"Thank you. Are you working tomorrow?"

"Yes, I'm here for the next few days."

"Good. I'll check in with you tomorrow to see how he is doing."

"Okay, see you then."

Arriving home late, Olivia took a long, warm shower, rinsing away the fatigue of the day. Dressing in capri sweats and an old T-shirt, she prepared herself some Havarti cheese, grapes, and crackers. She retrieved a bottle of white wine from the wine fridge and selected a large glass from the cabinet. For a brief second she thought of pouring a glass, but instead walked out to the deck with the entire bottle and the fruit and cheese plate. She sat down in her comfy patio chair overlooking the lake and drank in the beauty of the water. She poured a glass of wine and slowly took a sip, savoring the crisp, fruity flavor. It felt refreshing as the wine danced among her taste buds. Closing her eyes and letting out a loud sigh, she leaned back in the chair and started to relax.

Enjoying the cool breeze with a faint hint of warmth left over from the summer, her mind kept going over the events of the day. She couldn't shake the weird sensation of meeting Room 7's mother today. The feeling of having known this woman, the feeling of familiarity she just couldn't figure out. In the end she chalked it up to being tired from putting in too many hours. Her thoughts turned to Kev, remembering her dream last night. She got up from the chair and opened the sliding glass door. She walked into her bedroom and opened the top dresser of her underwear drawer, reached to the back, and removed a small brass compass. Holding it gently in her hands, she walked back to the patio, sat down, and held it tightly to her chest. Closing her eyes, she recalled feeling incredibly lonely back then. As the days went on without Kev she withdrew into herself, not caring what was going on. She moved around like a ghost of her old self. She felt like a wilted rose that was bent over from lack of water and sunshine. Her spirit cracked, dry and fragile, swaying to keep upright as if any minute she would drop, slowly falling into the dirt, to be finally swallowed by the earth.

She knew her parents worried about her and became frustrated that she wouldn't snap out of her sadness. *Snap out of it*, she would think, becoming infuriated. *How do you just snap out of it? My heart has completely been torn in two and is hanging in my chest by threads.* Most days she was fueled by anger. Anger at Kev for leaving, not ringing or writing or leaving a clue of where he went. It was easier to get through each day with anger instead of shuffling through the day with clouded vision and an ache so bad in her chest. She would often have to stop just to be able to breathe.

Many weeks after Kev had left, Olivia was in the family lounge of the pub with her family, cousins, and friends. Some relatives had come over from Leeton for a few days over the school holidays. Everyone was milling around talking, drinking beer, and grazing on sausage rolls, party-size meat pies, and chips that Johno had prepared that afternoon. The kids were over by the jukebox, taking turns selecting their favorite songs and drinking way too many soft drinks. Olivia was smiling and actually enjoying being with her cousins. Earlier they had walked up the street to look at the shops and buy lollies from the Garden of Roses Café. Olivia was cheerily listening to her cousin Kerri talk about the upcoming class excursion to Sydney and how she was hoping she'd get to sit next to a boy she liked. Kerri's cousin Leanne interrupted rudely like she always did. Olivia didn't like her, as she had never a nice thing to say. Her tiny dark eyes were set below her bushy black eyebrows that were constantly turned inward, as she was always frowning. She was short and round with the blackest, frizzy hair that surrounded her face like a Brillo pad. Olivia, who could always find the good in people, only found meanness in her.

"Hey Olivia, I heard your little boyfriend Kev left town. So what, did he finally get sick of hangin' out with a little kid like you?" Leanne said with a smirk on her face.

Olivia looked at her incredulously as Kerri said, "Now, Leanne, that was mean. Take it back."

Trying to look innocent and failing miserably, Leanne said, "Oh, I was just sayin', you know, what a spunk Kev was. I just thought since he was older than you that he probably was lookin' for a girl his own age."

Kerri, knowing how close Kev and Olivia were, intervened before Olivia could get a word out. "Shut up. You don't know anything, so keep your big gob shut."

Olivia could feel the heat rising into her face and the fury exploding behind her eyes. She started to stand and reach over the table, when her grandmother touched her on the shoulder, saying, "G'day girls, are you havin' a lovely time?"

Kerri and Leanne both pasted smiles on their faces and said in unison, "Yes, thank you."

"Good." Turning to Olivia, she said, "I need you to help me in the kitchen. Johno has left for the night."

"Yes, Grandmother," Olivia replied between gritted teeth, spearing Leanne with a murderous look as she turned and walked away. Walking out of the side double doors with her grandmother and feeling the cool air rush across her face, she let out a deep, audible sigh. She stormed off down the footpath, reaching a wooden column and hitting it with both her palms, crying out, "What a mean, ugly, bloody bitch!"

Grandmother calmly said, "I know she is a bloody bitch."

Quickly, she spun around to face her grandmother, her eyes wide and the fury of words halting on her lips. Olivia was too stunned to speak. She had never heard her grandmother swear and had fully expected to be chastised for swearing herself. Grandmother began to laugh after seeing the look on her face. "Come on, love, your grandmother knows a few swear words. Learn a few with hearing the blokes in the pub all these years. I don't like to use them, as they are not very ladylike. But in some instances, they are justly in need of use."

Smiling at her grandmother and losing some of the momentum of her anger, Olivia said, "Ah! I just wanted to scratch her eyes out."

"I know, and you probably would have if I hadn't interrupted. Was she goin' on about Kev?" Olivia nodded sadly. "That's what I thought. I was keepin' an eye on you and noticed that spiteful smirk on that horrible girl's face," she said as she reached Olivia and embraced her in a loving hug. Holding on tightly and letting out another sigh, Oliva felt herself deflate. The anger, now gone, was replaced with deep sadness. She heard her grandmother's voice muffled in her hair, "Come on, let's go back in. Don't let her ruin your time with your cousins."

Pulling back and looking into her grandmother's kind eyes, Olivia said, "I'll be back in. I need to have a few minutes alone."

"Alright, but don't be too long. I'll be looking for you."

Olivia headed for the stairs as Grandmother walked back into the family lounge. She reached the second floor verandah and walked into the upstairs foyer, looking around to make sure she was alone. She quickly rushed over to the fireplace, squeezed behind the couch, and sat down, leaning against the inside wall of the fireplace. She closed her eyes, slowed her breathing, and started to feel her entire body begin to relax. When she was little, this was her place to escape when she was scared. Now that she was older it became her place to relax and be alone.

She imagined she was down at the river with Kev, sitting on the river bank, running her fingers through the soft sand, starting with small circles, around and around, slowly widening from her body. As her left hand reached out farther, she brushed against something solid. The clinking sound of metal on the grate of the fireplace startled her from her reverie. Opening her eyes and reaching under the grate, her fingers touched something cold and metal. Leaning with her hand outstretched, she reached further under the grate, pulling out a round, brass, circular container with a note attached by a rubber band. Puzzled, Olivia slipped off the rubber band, the note falling into her lap. Suddenly realizing what she held in her hands, she gently found the small latch and opened the lid. She watched the small metal arm spring back and forth and finally still on southeast. A small gasp escaped her lips. She knew this was Kev's grandfather Poppy Bill's compass. After he passed last year he left it for Kev. It was his most valued possession. *What is it doing here?* she wondered. She reached for the note in her lap. Unfolding it with shaky hands, she read,

Dear Liv,

I don't know what's going on. Mum's taking us away for a bit, said Dad's in some kind of trouble and he wants us to go away until it's sorted out. I don't have a clue where we are going or for how long. All I know is I'll be back as soon as I can. I'll ring you.

I'm leaving you my Poppy Bill's compass so you'll know I'll be back. We will find our way back to each other. You keep it safe for me. I'd never leave it with anyone but you. My best mate. Now don't be sad and mope around like you do when you're down. Just be my Funny Face. I've got to hurry it up. I snuck out while Mum was running around the house. I didn't have time to ride to your house, so I'm leaving this in your secret place.

I'll miss you Liv.

Love, KeV

P.S. We won't be lost... we will find the right direction back to each other one day.

Tears slowly fell down her cheeks onto the letter, she kept reading the line, "Love, Kev." It sent an excited shiver through her. Kev loves me. Like love and not a best mate. Smiling and crying at the same time, she felt her heart swell as a small seed of hope had planted itself in her heart, taking root and beginning to bud.

Returning her thoughts to the present, she suddenly felt tired. Thinking of old memories always drained her energy. The sun was low in the sky as the faint rays cast a light pink haze over the water. Her eyes became very heavy, and she fought to keep them open. Gathering up the now empty dish, wine glass, and what was left of the wine, she took them inside. After rinsing the dish and glass, replacing the cork in the bottle, and placing it back in the fridge, she went back outside to retrieve the compass, then walked back to her bedroom and gently put it back in the drawer for safekeeping. She treasured the compass, as it was all she had left of Kev, but sometimes it angered her because it hadn't helped her in finding him.

Normally she would read for a while, but tonight she was too tired. She wearily climbed into bed after brushing her teeth and fell asleep almost immediately.

CHAPTER 6

Olivia was tossing and turning, tangling herself in the sheets. She was dreaming of running down the foyer stairs of the pub and bumping into someone. She caught her balance and looked up to the person's face to apologize. The person had dark brown eyes and shimmering charcoal hair—it was Kev's mum. Olivia sat up abruptly, gasping for air. She rubbed her eyes and covered her face with her hands, chanting "Oh my god, oh my god, it can't be." Rocking and trying to slow her breathing, she whispered, "Vic?" Shaking her head in an attempt to reach some sanity, she kept repeating, "No, it can't be." She convinced herself she was only dreaming of her childhood, which she did when she felt really lonely or stressed out. Taking a deep breath, she lay back upon the pillow and stared at the ceiling. As hard as she tried, she was unable to get the vision of Vic's face out of her mind.

She lay there for what seemed like hours trying to rationalize why this woman she had met today looked like Kev's mum Vic. Oh, it was probably just the bloody wine and being so tired. The woman didn't have the same last name as Vic. What was it she said? Olivia tried to recall. Yeah, Price, that's it. Ah, dreaming things up again, she thought as she plumped up the pillow, rolled onto her side, pulled the comforter up, and closed her eyes. A few minutes later her eyes flew open as she thought, Victoria Price, she said her name was Victoria. She went over and over this in her mind, putting it down to coincidence. Finally accepting this, she lay back down again, she couldn't get the picture of Kev's mum out of her mind, her face replaced by the beautiful, older Mrs. Price.

Exacerbated, she threw back the cover and said, "What the hell am I doing?" After quickly washing her face, brushing her teeth, and pulling her long wavy hair back in a band, she changed out of her nightie and dressed in her worn nursing scrubs.

She drove just over the speed limit along the road that circumvented the lake. It was still dark out with a hint of cool crispness in the early morning fall air. Shaking off a chill that caused her to shiver, she brushed it off as being cold and not false hope that had her clutching the steering wheel with both hands. She pulled into the nearly deserted parking lot, parked her sedan, and got out. The entire walk to the back entrance of the hospital, she kept admonishing herself, thinking, *I've finally lost it, I'm nuts, I've finally lost my mind. I'm wishing and wanting this bad enough that I've made this entire thing up in my mind.*

Pausing at the back entrance she stopped and thought, *Could Kev possibly be here?* Vic and Kev disappeared in the middle of summer in 1976, and she hadn't heard from them since. It was a big mystery to her back then. They had taken off in the night and no one would explain why they really left. No matter how hard Olivia tried to get information from her parents and grandparents she was always told the same thing: "We haven't heard from Vic and neither has Jimmy. We don't know." Her grandmother had always assured her that she would see him again one day. This belief had diminished in her heart as the years went by. She was never given an explanation and was secretly mad at Kev for leaving her. For weeks after he left she would ride by his old house, hoping by chance they had come back home. She finally gave up, realizing she would never see him again. Her broken heart never fully healed.

Olivia passed her badge in front of the key reader, opened the door, and walked into the deserted hallway. Scanning to make sure there was no one around, she reached the back stairwell and climbed to the second floor past the back of the nurse's station of telemetry. A tired-looking nurse looked up from the computer, saying, "Hey, Olivia, it's four in the morning. What are you doing here?"

Startled, she replied, "Oh, I've got a lot going on today, thought I would get a head start on things." Olivia knew she was a terrible liar and it would show on her face.

She kept her head down and continued walking to the unit. She heard the nurse call out, "Maybe if you had a boyfriend you wouldn't work so much."

The unit was dimly lit, as the lights had been turned down. She noticed a lot of activity in Room 4; the monitor alarms were dinging loudly. *Someone must not be doing well if everyone is in there,* Olivia thought. She quickly ducked to the left around the back of the nurse's station so she wouldn't have to pass by Room 4 and risk anyone seeing her. She didn't want to have to explain why she was at work at four in the morning.

Inhaling deeply and slowly letting her breath out to try and ease her nerves, she found the courage to open the door to Room 7 and walked in. As her eyes adjusted to the dark room, she heard the rhythmic hiss of the ventilator. Slowly crossing the room, she moved towards the head of the bed. She saw a male patient lying supine, with the head of the bed elevated the required thirty degrees to prevent brain swelling. As she crept closer, she placed her hands on the side rail and leaned in closer to see the patient's face. His eyes were closed; he had short wavy blonde hair. His skin was a little pale but didn't hide the light brown tan he had. She reached to touch his face, gently caressing his cheek down along his jawline, noticing the faint stubble of hair. Taking in all his features, she gasped, stepped back, and covered her mouth with her hands to stifle her disbelief. On shaking legs, she wobbled backwards and collapsed into the bedside chair. Tears began coursing down her face, and her heart was racing like it was going to burst from her chest.

"Kev?" she whispered.

Struggling to compose herself, she put down the bedside rail and scooted closer to the bed. She sat holding his hand, absorbing every detail of his beautiful face. She kept comparing images of him as a boy to this handsome man. He looked the same as she last saw him, only he had grown into a man. She estimated he was probably 6' 3" from what she could tell with him lying in the bed. He still had the long eyelashes, perfectly straight nose, and high cheekbones with a strong, masculine jawline. Her eyes fell to his full lips, wanting nothing more than to place hers on his. She didn't overlook how broad his shoulders were and his muscular chest and arms. His hand swallowed hers as she held it. She clutched him for dear life, for if she didn't, he may have disappeared.

"Oh, Kev," she whispered, "I missed you so much. I never thought I would ever see you again. I can't believe this is you. Why didn't you look for me? Why didn't you call? Where did you go?" Question after unanswered question raced through her mind until pure exhaustion overtook her. Without realizing it, she laid her head on his lower chest with his hand tightly in hers and fell asleep.

As she slept, Kev took his free hand and slowly reached down, gently moving the few strands of wavy hair that had escaped her ponytail from her face. He lovingly caressed her cheek as tears fell slowly down his face and onto the pillow.

CHAPTER 7

Suzanna was startled as she walked into Room 7. There was Olivia asleep with her head resting on the patient's chest. "Holy Moses," she whispered. "What in the world is she doing?" She walked over to her and placed a hand on her shoulder and gently shook her, "Wake up, Olivia, wake up." Olivia slowly stirred, opening her eyes and focusing on her surroundings. She looked up, confused, but when she saw the patient's face, reality quickly sank in. She hadn't been dreaming last night. This was so incredibly real. Here was Kev. Before she could go on asking herself a million questions, Suzanna interrupted her thoughts.

"Have you finally gone and lost your mind? I know you care about the patients, but what on earth are you doing sleeping with them? And, I mean, you are literally sleeping with a patient," Suzanna cried out.

"Shh, shh," Olivia said holding up her hands. "I'll explain."

"Darn right you will."

Standing up, Olivia reached for Suzanna's arm. "Come with me now." Suzanna followed her out of the room and into the clean utility room. As the door closed, Olivia turned to face her. "It's Kev! That patient in there is Kev," she shouted, hardly believing herself.

"What? Kev? As in your missing Kev?"

"Yes, that's him. He is here."

"Are you sure? It could be someone that looks like him."

"No, it's him. I know it's been sixteen years, but that's him. He hasn't changed that much, his looks have changed into an older version of himself. I can't believe it, I've found Kev."

"Well I'll be darned."

"I know, I can't believe it. After all this time," she said as she gave her a hug. Stepping back, Olivia excitedly explained, "I've got to find his mother. I've got to know what happened. Where did they go? Why didn't he ever contact me?"

"Slow down. First thing, you need to go home, shower, and eat something. Mrs. Price doesn't usually visit in the mornings. She has some type of work at Kev's office. She's always here around five. It'll give you time to calm down a bit so you won't go off half-cocked with all of your questions."

"No! Well, yes, I'll shower and eat, then I'm going to Kev's office. I've waited all these years; I'm not waiting any-more. I'll find out what happened if it's the last thing I do."

Knowing Olivia had made up her mind, Suzanna didn't try to convince her otherwise. "Do you even know where his office is or what his business is called?"

"As a matter of fact, I do. It's on the face sheet of his demographics," she replied, smiling. "Before I do, I'm going to go back in and sit with him for a while. I don't want to leave him just yet." Returning to his room, she noted it was brighter now; the sun was shining through the large window. Sunlight was filtered across the room, sending a soft light over his face. *Wow*, she thought, *he's even more handsome than he was early this morning.* His features were more defined, revealing his strong jawline and long eyelashes. She sat next to him and held his hand, still not believing it was actually him. She sat there for over an hour, telling him of her life after he had left. She wasn't sure if he could hear her, but it felt good to talk to him.

Olivia was startled when the privacy curtain was torn back viciously, revealing Victoria Price. Before Olivia could gather her wits, Victoria said firmly, "What are you doing near my son? Get out!"

Olivia stood up confused, "What do you mean, Victoria? It's me, Olivia, Olivia Clark."

"I know who you are."

"Then I don't understand. I thought you'd be happy to see me. It's been years. I've missed Kev for so long; why didn't he ever contact me?"

"Because I told him you were dead," she replied cruelly.

Stunned, Olivia felt like she had been punched in the guts and the wind knocked out of her. "You! You what?"

"Oh, stop blabbering. When we left that miserable town, I didn't look back. I didn't want Kev ever going back there and living some godforsaken life with you. He would have rotted in that place. I wanted him to have a life, a good life. That town, the people are his past, and that's exactly what you are, the past."

The reality of what she was hearing sank in. Fueled by anger, she walked over to Victoria and stood inches from her face, "You cruel, fucking bitch," she seethed.

Victoria stepped back. "You don't get to speak to me like that. You are just a stupid, country girl born in the bush. Now leave. Kev wouldn't want to see you; he has his own life now. He probably doesn't even remember you."

Fists clenching at her sides and red heat flushing her face, Olivia said, "Kev should have been able to make up his own mind. You robbed him of that chance, our friendship," she shrieked as her voice started to rise.

Laughing, Victoria said, "Oh, look at you, all heartbroken over a boy you knew as a child. Grow up and leave the past in the past where it belongs."

Olivia looked at the screen. Kev's heart rate was high in the 150s. "Go get Suzanna the nurse, hurry!" she screamed at Victoria. Victoria stood there defiantly with a smug look on her face. "Aren't you going to get the nurse?" Olivia cried out incredulously as Suzanna and Hazel ran into the room. Suzanna did a quick assessment on Kev, noting his heart rate was coming down.

Suzanna glanced at Olivia's pained expression and noticed all the color had gone from her face. "Hey, Olivia, he's okay, just a short burst of tachycardia. I think his sedation has worn off and he is getting a little agitated."

"Yes, he's agitated alright, if he heard the conversation that was had in here," Olivia remarked as she brushed past Victoria, searing her with a furious look, and walked out the door. Suzanna stood there confused, sensing something was very wrong.

Returning to her office, Olivia let out a pent-up breath and closed the door. She sat at her desk as if in a fog. Her emotions were so brittle, she felt like any moment she would shatter into a million tiny pieces. After booting up her computer and making several attempts to focus on her work, she gave up and started sobbing into her hands. Heart-wrenching sobs suppressed for years came roaring out as if breaking through a crumbling wall. She sat there for several minutes choking on years of unshed tears.

Several minutes later, she heard a faint knock on her door. Reaching for a Kleenex to blow her nose and dry her eyes, she thought if she was really quiet, whoever was there would think she was gone and would go away. The knocking grew louder and more persistent, then she heard Suzanna calling her name. Composing herself, Olivia got up and opened the door. Suzanna rushed in the door and closed it behind her. "What the hell went on in there? You're a complete wreck!"

"AHH!" Olivia screamed softly as she balled her hands into fists and shook them at her sides. "That heartless, crazy bitch had told Kev I was dead. Dead! How in the hell do you lie to your own son about that? She's fucking insane. I can't believe it. For Christ's sake, she was friends with my parents. She came to family dinners and get-togethers. It makes no sense. She won't allow me to see him. She makes his decisions while he is incapacitated. I don't believe this. Suzanna, he is laying in that fucking hospital bed and I can't go in and see him."

"Calm down and take a breath. Look, I'll sneak you in when she's not here and keep guard in case she shows up. Don't worry about it, we'll figure it out."

"No, we won't. She said he won't want to see me, that he probably doesn't even remember who I am," Olivia said as fresh tears began flowing down her face.

Suzanna reached for her arm. "You have no idea what he would want or thinks. I wouldn't believe a word his mother says. I beg you to wait until he wakes up; I'm sure he will very much want to see you."

"I don't know, Suzanna. I'm so exhausted. This has been an emotional roller coaster ride for me the past few days. I'm going to go home and get some rest. I'll figure out how to deal with her and I'll pray for Kev to wake up. Keep me posted."

"Alright, I'll talk to you tomorrow. Get some rest. I'll take good care of him for you," Suzanna said as she walked out the door.

CHAPTER 8

Olivia could faintly hear the pounding on her door. Ignoring it as she had the past two days, she rolled over and put a pillow over her head. A few moments later the pounding stopped. *Peace and quiet at last,* she thought fleetingly as the bedroom lights suddenly came on. Startled, Olivia sat up squinting from the sharp, bright light. Standing in the doorway was Suzanna with a look of relief on her face that was quickly replaced with concerned anger.

"Olivia," Suzanna yelled, "You've had me worried sick for the past two days, you haven't been to work, calling in sick, not answering your phone or answering the door. For God's sake, I thought you were dead."

"I haven't been feeling well, they would have told you that at work. Now turn off the lights, I'm trying to rest. And the door key I gave you was for emergencies only."

"Good Lord, it stinks in here." Suzanna stomped over to the windows, throwing back the drapes, pulling up the blinds, and opening the windows. "And this is an emergency. When I normally talk to you every day, but can't reach you in days, then there's something wrong. Geez, you never take off work this long. If anything, you never leave the place. So yeah, in my book this is an emergency. Now get out of bed and get in the shower while I fix you something to eat."

"No," she replied.

"Oh no, you don't want to test me right now. This country girl has hogtied a few hogs in her life, and I'm not opposed to doing that to you. Now get out of that bed!"

Olivia could tell by the look on her face that she meant it. "Okay, okay, I'm getting up," she said.

She staggered into the bathroom. Looking at herself in the mirror, she gasped in horror. *Oh, I look like shit*, she thought. Large, dark circles under her eyes, her hair limp with layers of grease. Inhaling, she almost gagged. "Cripes, I do stink." She stripped down and got in the shower.

After brushing her teeth twice and brushing the tangles from her hair, she dressed and shuffled out to the kitchen in an old pair of sweatpants and a T-shirt. Suzanna looked her over and said, "Much better, now sit down. I've made you tomato soup and a grilled cheese sandwich. It's all I could find in your barren refrigerator." Olivia did as she was asked, not making eye contact with her. Suddenly, she felt a wave of guilt wash over her for making Suzanna worry so much. They sat in silence until Olivia had eaten all of the soup and sandwich. Taking the dishes to the sink, Suzanna got two steaming mugs of coffee and said, "Come on, let's go sit outside on the deck."

Olivia sat down on one of the patio chairs, brought her knees up, and cradled her coffee between them as she hugged her knees, grasping the coffee mug to help warm her up. Ever since the confrontation with Victoria, she felt constantly chilled. All she could feel were shards of icicles coursing through her blood.

Suzanna was the first to break the silence. "It's been hard to deal with Kev's mother. She's been very demanding and controlling, more so now that she knows about you."

"Selfish fucking bitch!" Olivia spat out, becoming angry all over again.

"Yeah, she is, and there's something not right about her."

"I'm still getting over the shock of actually finding him and the fact that he is sick. I'm so scared I won't get to talk to him and he won't know I'm alive. And to top it all off, she won't let me in to see him. I want to fucking kill her. Strangle her neck until her eyes fall out of her psycho head."

"I don't blame you," Suzanna said as she started to smile.

"What are you smiling about? I'm sitting here confessing to a homicide I want to commit and you're sitting there like I told you a funny joke."

Holding up her hand waving in surrender, "I'm sorry. I'm just so excited to tell you that he is asking to see you."

Startled, spilling her coffee down her thighs, Olivia looked at Suzanna with a total look of surprise. Stammering, Olivia said, "Kev's awake? He's talking? He wants to see me? How does he know I'm alive or even here?"

Suzanna cut her off, knowing her endless questioning would never cease. "Yes, he's awake, and yes, he can talk. He's been in and out of consciousness since your first visit when you found him. He knew that was you. He is just as stunned as you were to see you in his room. He told me he thought he was hallucinating from all the drugs he had been given. He is threatening to get out of bed and come find you himself."

Shocked into silence, Olivia couldn't believe he was awake and she could actually talk to him.

"Now that he is awake, you can go see him. His mother has no say now. He can make his own decisions. What are you waiting for? Stop sitting there crying like a baby, you can finally go see him."

Olivia jumped up. "You're right, come on, let's go."

"Uh, you might want to go fix yourself up a bit. You may smell better, but you look awful."

"Thanks a lot," she said, smiling as she ran in to repair the damage two tear-stained days had inflicted on her. As she was about to walk out of the house, she ran back to the bedroom.

"Where are you going?" Suzanna called out.

As she reached for the compass in the top drawer, Olivia whispered, "To get the one thing that's allowed me to have hope."

CHAPTER 9

As Suzanna drove Olivia to the hospital, Olivia was a nervous, anxious mess, constantly clenching her hands around the compass and peppering Suzanna with questions. "Do you think he'll care about me the same way he did when we were kids? Will he have changed that much?"

"Olivia, stop! You are driving me and yourself insane. Stop with the crazy questions." Squeezing her hand and softening her tone, she reassured Olivia, "I talked with Kev, and by the state he was in after confronting his mother for lying about you, I'd say that man has never forgotten you. I'd bet my life on it that he still loves you and the years that you shared."

"But we were just kids, what did we know about love?"

Sighing, Suzanna replied, "I can't explain the affairs of the heart. What I do know is you both shared a very strong connection that time and absence could never sever. Now calm down. Do you want him to see you as a raving lunatic?"

Taking slow, deep breaths to help ease her dizziness, Olivia said, "I'm just so scared, Suzanna."

"Yeah, I know."

Suzanna pulled away from the back entrance as Olivia was walking in the door to the hospital. Taking the back stairwell again to avoid running into anyone, she moved quickly up the stairs. Her heart was racing and her belly felt like it was full of butterflies. She exited the stairwell on the second floor and looked around to make sure she didn't run into anyone. Right now she could not summon up a simple conversation, she was too nervous. It was after 4:30 in the afternoon, so most of the activity had died down, as doctors had already rounded and many had left for the day. She was able to make it into the ICU without running into anyone until she rounded the corner of the nurse's station. She was met with a few strange glances from the nurses. *Oh shit, what do they know?* Olivia thought.

Walking quickly past them, she walked up to Room 7 just as Ronnie came out. Smiling, Ronnie said, "He's waiting for you."

Smiling weakly, Olivia pushed open the door. Thankfully, Ronnie had pulled the curtain to keep them from prying eyes. She walked around the curtain, stepping up to the bed. Tears sprang to her eyes as she saw Kev sitting up in bed, fully alert and handsome as ever, smiling that cheeky smile he always reserved for her. He held out his arms and simply said one word full of emotion: "Livie." Whatever reservations or fear she had completely dissolved. She ran to the bed and fell into his arms. Holding on to him for dear life and with his arms around her, they both cried.

Tears of love, friendship, separation, and joy all rushed out like a dam had finally burst and the wall had finally crumpled.

Kev pulled back, cradling her face in his hands, "Let me look at you. You're just as I remember, only you have grown into yourself." He let out a low whistle. "You are so beautiful." Blushing, Olivia looked down. "You haven't changed, you still blush just like when we were kids," he said. Looking down at her clenched fist, she slowly opened it, revealing the compass. "Well I'll be damned, that's Pop's compass," Kev exclaimed. "You held onto it for all these years?"

"Of course I did. It was the one thing that held me to you. I've said a few swear words to it over the years. I thought it was broken 'cause I couldn't find the right direction to find you."

"Somehow it did the trick. You've found me, Liv." She lunged into his arms again and held him tight, snuggling her face gently into his chest. Caressing his fingers through her soft, long hair, he smelled its sweet scent. He whispered, "We have a lot to talk about."

"I know. Will you just hold me for now?"

"I'm never letting you go," he said as fresh tears began streaming down his face.

CHAPTER 10

A few days later Oliva entered Kevin's room and was surprised to see him sitting up in a chair, finishing his breakfast. "Wow, you look great."

"You trying to flirt with a sick man, Liv?" he said mischievously.

"Don't flatter yourself. That was purely from a medical perspective," she quipped back. Smiling, she walked over to him and placed a kiss on his cheek and sat beside him. "Seriously, how do you feel?"

"Pretty good, my counts are normal. The pneumonia is gone. A bit of a cough. I'm still weak, but I feel ready to go home."

"Maybe they'll let you out in the next couple of days."

"Hope so. You gonna be my private nurse?"

"Maybe I can, since we have more catching up to do. I still can't believe you became an architect. You were terrible at making our forts when we were kids. They always fell down."

"I was not. I just had a bad contractor who didn't follow directions well."

"I think there's meds still in your system, 'cause you aren't remembering very well."

"Oh no, I do remember very well. Remember when we were at the old Brindabella Station? You left me with the Brindabella kids and ran off with Aubrey to sunbake. You two climbed up onto the roof of the wool shed out back, laid down your towels, took your tops off, and slathered baby oil all over yourselves."

Olivia's cheeks began to burn as a flame of red heat rushed up her face. Kev chuckled, "Yeah, topless sunbaking. What, were you trying to bring Bondi Beach to the bush? 'Cause I gotta say, I liked the idea." He was thoroughly enjoying watching her squirm with embarrassment.

Olivia leaned forward in her chair and exclaimed, "You bloody little perv, I thought you went down to the river to fish for yabbies with the boys."

"I knicked back to the house for more bait, saw you two on the shed and couldn't resist a peek. I climbed onto the tool shed, and almost broke my neck when I saw you with no top on." Kev let out a low, whooshing breath. "Bloody hell, Liv, what a great sight, every boy's dream," he said with a barely contained grin.

"Oh stop, I can't believe you," she said as she threw a wadded-up napkin at him, barely missing his head. At that moment, the physical therapist walked in: a pencil-thin man, around forty, with a bald head and squinty eyes.

"Good morning. I'm Leroy, I'll be working with you today, since Will is on vacation."

"Mornin', Leroy, my friend and I were just talking about old times," said Kev.

"Lots of good memories, I'm sure."

"Oh, you wouldn't believe how good they were," he said as he looked over at Olivia and saw the look she was giving him. The look that meant "I will kill you," as he remembered from their childhood. Leroy, distracted said, "I completely forgot the walker; you're going to be doing a few laps today. I'll be right back," he said as he walked out the door.

Kev looked sheepishly at Olivia, who really didn't look that miffed at all. For some reason she looked a little amused. As she stood up to leave, she said, "Well, this had been a great trip down memory lane, you little perv, but I've got to run. I'll be back later to check on you." She bent down and gave him a quick peck on the cheek, noting that he didn't feel warm. No fever.

Kev smiled up at her. "I'll see you later, Funny Face." She stopped in her tracks with a sudden flashback to her childhood. She felt a sudden surge of warmth and love that she hadn't felt in so long—she had not been called that in years. She walked to the door, then turned back to look at him. She mischievously smiled at him and said, "Oh, Kev, that day on the shed." He looks at her quizzically.

"I knew you were watching." And she walked out the door smiling.

She heard him laughing out, "You little tart."

As she left the intensive care unit via the double doors, she ran into Shirley, who had a perpetual scowl on her face. Shirley looked at her and said, "What are you smiling about?"

Olivia replied dreamily, "I was thinking how nice it would be to be outside tanning in the warm sun," and continued on her way.

Shirley looked at her retreating back, shook her head, and called after her, "Don't you know it's raining out there?"

CHAPTER 11

They sat beside the window overlooking the lake. It was an overcast morning with enormous, dark clouds rolling in from the west, moving in slowly, with the rain threatening to fall at any moment. Sipping her coffee, Olivia said, "I love mornings like this. I never tire of watching the rain fall and the ripples they make on the water."

"Yeah, I haven't seen a good rain in a while. We need to go outside and smell the air. Nothin' like the earthy scent of rain falling on the dry soil," Kev replied.

"Or lying in bed listening to the rain falling on the tin roof of the Commercial Pub."

"I remember those nights when you, Kerri, and I would have sleepovers and fall asleep to the rain pattering on the tin roof."

"Speaking of Kerri, I talked to her yesterday. She's still pretty spun out about you and everything that has happened this week. She can't believe we just fell into each other's laps. She went on about it being something like fate and meant to be."

"I don't care what she calls it, I'm just happy it happened," he said as he reached for her hand. They both turned their heads toward the direction of the door as they heard Dr. Breland walk in. "Good morning, Mr. Anderson, Miss Clark."

"Morin," Kev replied, thinking this bloke needed to lighten up. He was so formal and uptight; thankfully he was a great oncologist.

"I've reviewed your morning laboratory results and chest X-ray. Everything is within normal limits. You have progressed exceedingly well with physical therapy. You have made an excellent recovery, much faster than expected. I'm discharging you today. Do you have any questions?"

Grinning, Kev answered, "Nah, Doc, sign the papers, and I'll be outta here."

"Very well. I'll complete the necessary discharge papers. Make an appointment with my office for next week. The nurse will make the arrangements for you to leave." He nodded, turned, and walked out of the room.

Kev reached over and pulled Olivia onto his lap, hugging her tightly. He sighed happily. "Where you takin' me, Livie?"

"Well, if you want my private duty nursing skills, I don't think it's a good idea to go back to your house. Especially after the outburst your mother had."

"Yeah, you're right. She'd have way too much access to my house. She'd be comin' over all the time, making our lives hell, especially yours."

"Yes, she made her opinion of me very clear."

"Let's not worry about her. I can deal with her later. I'll stay with you, and you can wait on me hand and foot."

Nudging him in the ribs, she chuckled. "I don't think so."

Later, Olivia pulled the car up to the side entrance of the hospital as Suzanna and Kev walked out the doors. She got out of the car and walked over to Kev, who was standing there inhaling deeply.

"Smell that, Liv? The rain's coming."

"I know. It smells so fresh and clean. Come on, we better hurry up before it unleashes and we get drenched." Once belted in the car, they said goodbye to Suzanna. Kev thanked her for all of her care. "I'll ring you later," Olivia called out as she pulled away from the curb.

Stirring the marinara sauce, she was interrupted by the ringing of the phone, "Hello."

"Hey, Cuz, how's it goin'?"

"Hi Kerri, everything is great. No, more than great. It's fantastic."

"So I s'pose you and Kev are hittin' it off?"

"It's crazy. It's like there was no time apart, we have picked up from where we left off. Nothing's changed, we get along like we used to."

"That's great. So what are your plans now that you two are back together?"

"I don't know. We've only been home for two weeks now. Kev is back to health, he wants to start back to work next week. We're taking one day at a time," she said as she glanced out of the kitchen window. She saw Kev with a grim look, shaking his head as he said something on his mobile phone.

"You still there, Liv?"

"Oh yeah, Kev's outside on the phone. From the looks of it, he must be talking to his mother."

"That whacko still givin' ya grief?"

"Yes, she insists he give up this little romantic fantasy of the past and leave me. At least at my house she can't come barging over, so thankfully I don't have to deal with her."

"Cripes. You two should move back here."

"In a roundabout way, we have talked about it. We both reminisce about living in Hay. How we both loved growing up in that little bush town. I miss being able to walk up the street to the shops or go to the park and see the peacocks and roos roaming around."

"Well, maybe one day soon you'll get tired of livin' with the Yanks and come back home."

"Hopefully. Hey, I'm gonna let you go. Kev's off the phone and I'm making his tea."

"Alright, I'll ring you later. See ya. Say hi to Kev for me."

"Bye." She had already hung up. She replaced the phone in the cradle as he walked in through the patio doors. She could see he was trying to collect his anger. Smiling she said, "Kerri just called; she said to say hi."

"Ahh, good. How she goin'?"

"She's well, still the same old Kerri."

Nodding he replied, "I'm gonna hit the shower, I won't be long."

Olivia returned to the stove to check on the sauce and start the water for the pasta. About twenty minutes later she could smell the masculine fragrance of pine and oak as Kev walked into the kitchen.

CHAPTER 12

Turning from the sink, Olivia bumped into Kev, chest to chest. Olivia said with a hint of annoyance, "Come on, move it. How am I supposed to make you your favorite meal when you are in the way?"

As she tried to step around him, Kev stopped her by catching her around the waist. She turned her head up to look at him. He looked deep into her eyes for several seconds, then leaned down slowly and gently kissed her lips. This caught her by surprise, and for a second she didn't react. Kev pulled her closer, holding her in his arms, and began to kiss her more passionately. He gently pried her mouth open with his tongue and kissed her more urgently.

A sudden passion ignited in her as she placed her arms around his neck and sank deeper into his kiss. They both searched each other's mouths, exploring with their tongues and gently nipping the other's lips. Both of them moaned softly as they slowly pulled away and looked in wonder at each other. Kev leaned down and gave her one more passionate kiss. Holding her in his arms, he gave her a cheeky smile. Olivia was breathless. "Whoa, where did that come from?"

Kev confessed, "I've been wanting to kiss you like that since I was thirteen, but most recently when you first walked into my hospital room."

Smiling, she said, "We did try it once when we were around eleven. Remember, we were curious how to do it and you made a big mess of it by slobbering all over my face."

"Me! You were the one sucking and drooling," he laughed.

She whispered, "Well, it's a good thing you have improved, because that was very impressive."

His voice deepened as he replied, "Maybe we should try it again. You know, just to make sure we have it right this time."

Olivia reached up on her tiptoes and caressed his face with her hands, looking deeply into those beautiful blue eyes that reflected the lifetime of love they had for each other.

They held on tight, feeling as if letting go would sever their lifeline once again. All thoughts of dinner were forgotten. Kev reached behind her and turned the stove off, then took her hand and led her to the bedroom.

They stood beside the bed, kissing feverously while pulling, unzipping, and discarding their clothes. He picked her up and laid her on the bed. Crawling up on his knees, he stared down at her. His eyes were ablaze and her skin was flushed, her breathing erratic. Groaning, he bent his head and started kissing her again, exploring her body with his mouth. Her hands roamed across his body, feeling the hardness of his muscles over his sculpted form. They desperately sought to get closer to one another. The years of love and separation had built a greater need that was nearing the boiling point. Olivia reached over to turn off the lamp. Kev caught her hand and whispered, "Leave it on. I want to see you all of you."

Olivia was normally modest and shy, but not at this moment with Kev. This felt right, like she had been waiting her entire life for him. As he took her nipple in his mouth, all conscious thoughts disappeared. All that existed were the two of them and their love that had lived within them for the past two and a half decades.

Both sated, warm, and tingling with sweat, they lay in one another's arms. Olivia lay with her head on his chest, loving the feeling of his strong arms around her. Kev sighed.

"I can't believe all these years I thought you were dead. Fucking oath! What was my mother thinking? I'm so angry with her right now. All these years we could have been together."

"I don't understand it either. I don't want to talk about it just yet. I want to lay here in your arms and enjoy each other. You holding me makes me feel whole again. I always felt like something was missing in my life all these years, and that something was you."

Kev leaned up and rolled over, causing Olivia to roll onto her back. He stared down at her and said, "I have loved you my entire life, whether you were alive or not. You were always a part of me. I've missed you so much. I can't believe you are here now. I've fallen in love with you all over again. You are my Funny Face."

With tears in her eyes, she said, "I love you so much. I don't ever want to be without you again. I wouldn't survive." He leaned down and kissed her tenderly, then rolled onto his back, taking her with him.

Olivia woke up to the sun peeking in through the blinds. Opening her eyes, she found Kev smiling at her. Her heart skipped a beat and swelled with love and happiness. They were finally together again. "Mornin', sleepy head, thought you'd never wake up," he said.

"What! You kept me up all night! For a sick man, you certainly have a lot of stamina," she exclaimed as she elbowed him in the ribs.

"I'm feeling better, just wait 'til I get all my strength back," he laughed.

"Oh, God help me," she moaned as she covered her face with her hands.

He reached for her, "Oh come over here, love." With her head on his chest and his arms around her, she felt so utterly happy, she could barely stifle a giggle.

"Kev."

"Hmm?"

"Do you remember why you call me your Funny Face?"

"Of course I do."

"When you call me that, so many great memories come flooding back to me from when we were kids. I miss the times with my parents, grandparents, aunts, uncles, and cousins. They were such a big part of my life, and now I never hear from them. It's sad how we grow up and move on with our own lives, and the people who meant so much to us and influenced our lives are not here to share it."

"Yeah, I know. It's the reality of growing up. People move on and become so caught up with families of their own. Life becomes too busy. We had some pretty great times, though, didn't we? Remember your parents had that big family reunion in the ballroom of the Commercial?"

"Oh yeah, everyone came. The adults were laughing, drinking, smoking, and dancing. We all were having such a great time. Us kids got to run around the place, we stayed up really late, we sang and danced all night long. We even got to sleep in the double rooms, just us kids, four to a bed, sleeping head to toe. What were we, around eight or nine?"

"I think we were right around eight. Your uncle Henry manned the record player and wouldn't let anyone near it. Man, he must have played everything from Slim Dusty to Rod Stewart, ABBA, the Beatles, and my special favorite, Men at Work."

"I know. It was so much fun, we had the time of our lives. I learnt to pull my first beer from the bar tap. Dad taught me how to tilt the glass just right, so as not to get too much head of foam on top. I think I poured at least a dozen or more beers that night." She giggled. "Oh, and I was pouring scotch for Poppy Tom, and Grandfather roused on me for putting too much in the glass. So I tipped it down the sink to start over. I thought Grandfather was going to keel over right then. His face got so beet red as he couldn't believe I tipped his good scotch down the sink," she said, laughing. "My barmaid skills grinded to a halt for the night. Remember, Grandmother requested 'YMCA' by the Village People, and all of us kids lined up behind her. She showed us how to do the YMCA and we were all so into it."

Kev laughed, "Oh yeah. That was fun."

"It's fun to stay… at the YMCA," Olivia sang out.

"Still can't carry a tune, can ya?" joked Kev.

Ignoring him, she said, "We did all the motions with our arms, forming them into letters, following Grandmother's lead. It was so funny trying to stay in sync with each other. We finally got it down towards the end."

Laughing, Kev managed to say, "I can see it now. I thought you girls had all gone bloody mad. Then when he played

Sheena Easton you were struttin' your stuff all over the dance floor. Ouch, that hurt!" he said, smiling as she punched him in the arm.

"The part I will always remember is when the adults slow danced to Funny Face. It was so sweet and romantic. The entire atmosphere changed when that song played."

"That was one of the biggest hits in the early seventies, wasn't that by Donna Fargo?"

"Yeah, I think so. I just remember how the song made me feel so happy. I wanted to be Funny Face 'cause she was loved so much. I still have the 45 Mum and Dad gave me. I was always blaring it on the radio when it came on, so they bought me the record," she fondly recalled.

Kev started to sing to her:

Funny Face, I love you
Funny Face, I need you
My whole world is wrapped up in you
When the road I walk seems all uphill
And the colors in my rainbow all turn blue
You kiss my tears away
You smile at me and say:
Funny Face, Funny Face, I love you

They both belted out the final line. Their voices trailed off and they didn't finish the rest of the chorus, as they started making love again.

CHAPTER 13

Sitting with his mother in her home office, Kev had finished discussing the final plans for a new office building he was working on. Placing the plans aside, his mother asked, "How are you feeling?"

"I feel great, better than ever, thanks to Liv."

Seeing the smile fall from her face, he inwardly recoiled, as he knew what was coming. Why couldn't he remember to never mention her name around his mother? Then a thought suddenly occurred to him: he was well and truly in love with her. She was his past, and now she was his future. Standing, he walked over to the windows that faced the garden. "Mum, whatever you have against Liv, you're going to have to try and let it go."

"Kevin, I will not have you tell me what I will and will not do. I have my own reasons to despise that horrible girl."

"What, what reasons?" his voice rising. "What in the bloody hell has she ever done to you?"

"Calm down, Kevin."

"I won't calm down. Understand this: I'm in love with her, I'm going to spend the rest of my life with her. There is nothing you can do about it. Please just be happy for me."

"Do you really think it's wise to get so involved? You know, with your health problems?"

"For Christ's sake, Mother, I don't care. Even if I only get a short time with her, it will be worth it. I'm finally the happiest I've ever been."

"Oh, Kevin, we have been happy, haven't we?"

"Yes Mum, but you know this is different."

Noting his mother's eyes were a shade darker than normal and her face was drawn tight, he couldn't shake a feeling of impending doom. As quick as he felt this, he dismissed it as absurdity. Walking over to him, she said, "I want you to be happy. I'll try to not be so disparaging, and I will try to get used to the idea of you two together. Don't forget about your Mother. I still need my time with you."

Hugging her, he said, "It's alright, Mum, you're not losing me. We'll talk later. I've got something really important I need to do." She walked him to the door and waved to him as he drove away.

He rushed excitedly into the kitchen after parking the car. "Liv, Liv, I'm home." Not hearing her, he walked through the living room to the sliding glass door. He saw her standing at the end of the deck looking over the water in her winter jacket and hat.

He quietly walked up behind her and wrapped his arms around her waist. She smiled and leaned into him as he kissed her neck. Giggling, she said, "You better hurry up. My boyfriend will be home soon."

"He will, will he? Well then, you better turn around and give me a kiss." She turned to him and linked her arms around his neck. He leaned down and placed his lips on hers softly at first, then more firmly. He leaned away, pressing lighter kisses on her cheeks, eyelids, and lips. He pulled her closer, delving his tongue deeper in her mouth. Nibbling her lower lip, he heard a moan escape her mouth. Desire consumed him as he trailed kisses slowly down her neck. They both were exhaling quick, short breaths.

"Livie, I love you."

"I love you too," she moaned breathlessly.

Pulling away from her, he placed both hands on her face and looked into her eyes, "I feel like nothing is missing anymore, we finally have each other. All I want is for us to be together for the rest of our lives. Olivia, will you marry me?"

"Yes." Squealing in delight, she reached up and kissed him, "Yes."

He picked her up and twirled her around, both of them laughing happily. He sat her back on her feet. He took her left hand in his and placed a white-gold emerald-cut diamond ring on her finger. "Oh, Kev, it's beautiful."

Kissing her, he said, "Who said dreams can't come true?"

"That would have been me a few months ago."

"Never stop believing, Liv," he whispered as he picked her up and carried her into the house.

CHAPTER 14

As Olivia waited beside the window in the living room for her call to be answered, she heard the loud noise of a lot of people talking in the background. "Hello! Kerri, you there?"

"Hold on, it's loud in here. I'll go outside," said Kerri. Olivia waited as she heard footsteps and a door closing. "Hey, I'm back. I couldn't hear you in there," said Kerri.

"Where are you?" Olivia asked.

"I'm at the Griffith Art Gallery. I have a viewing this week."

"Oh, that's wonderful, I'm so happy for you."

"Thanks, Cuz. What's going on?"

"We're coming home in two weeks—we're getting married there!" Olivia replied.

"What! You just got engaged a month ago. That's quick, Liv."

"I know, but we don't see the point in waiting. We know we want to be together. There's no need to wait any longer. Plus, his mother will be out of town at that time. It will be so much easier for us to get away. We won't have to deal with her hysterics or her scheming to prevent us from going."

"The psycho still trying to break you two up?" Kerri groaned.

"Yes. She does make things difficult, but we ignore her attempts."

"What are your plans?"

"I was hoping I could email you all the details and what I'll need you to help me with."

"Sounds like I'm going to be busy," sighed Kerri.

"I know, I hate to ask. I know you are busy. I promise I'll keep the list of to-dos to a minimum."

"No worries. I have some downtime in the next few weeks, now that I've finished with the last of the showings."

"Oh, thank you. I owe you big time."

"It will be fun. I can't wait to see you two again, it's been way too long."

"I know, I'm so excited to go home, get married, and see you."

"How are you going to keep this from crazy?"

"We have to be very careful. I'll keep the things we need to bring for the wedding at Suzanna's house. Not that she comes to my house, I'm just being extra cautious. All communication and our itinerary will be on my computer."

"Good thinking. There's no telling what she'll do if she finds out."

"Oh, she can never find out. She'd probably kill me."

"Joking aside, Olivia, she really would off you. Be careful. Well, I've got to go. I'll wait for your email and will then get things going. See ya."

"Bye," Olivia said. "And thank you again," she added as she heard the dial tone.

PART II

CHAPTER 15

Olivia opened the door to see Suzanna, as she had expected. They had arranged to visit to catch up on the details of her trip to Australia and hear all about the wedding.

Suzanna reached out to hug Olivia. "Hello, Mrs. Anderson, how is the new bride?"

Squeezing her tight, Olivia replied, "It was more than I had ever dreamed of." She turned to the foyer, waving her hand. "Come on in, I've made coffee and have all the photos developed. Laughing, she said, "I almost thought I was going to run out of film. I used the entire fifteen rolls I brought with me."

Suzanna said, "Oh no, I'm going to be here all day!"

"No, I'll give you the short and skinny. We did so much in only two weeks. I can't believe it was real."

"Where is Kev?"

"He went to see his mother. He is not sure what to expect, since we did sneak out of the country to get married. She was furious with us."

"I'm surprised she didn't fly over there and try to stop you."

"We didn't give her time. Kerri and I had made all the arrangements before we left here. I gave her the instructions and she did all the hard work."

"I know you told me you were leaving to get married. I'm relieved you didn't tell me any details, because Victoria did question me about where you were. I could honestly tell her I didn't know."

"I thought she would harass my friends; that's why I told no one except you that we were going somewhere. She found out that we were out of town but didn't know where. Even if she discovered we were in Australia she wouldn't have made it, as we were married two days after arriving. Come on, let's go into the living room and I'll tell you all about it."

Both settled on the couch, coffee mugs in hand and stacks of photos neatly piled on the coffee table. Olivia started from the beginning. "After arriving in Sydney, we caught a domestic flight to Griffith, rented a car, and drove an hour and a half to Hay. It was surreal, seeing Hay, the Main Street and the old pub, the Commercial Hotel. After all these years it brought back so many good memories. We both were happy to be back. Exploring the town took us back in time to when we were kids; we ran around the town with not a care in the world back then. Oh, I could go on and on, but let me get to the wedding. We were married on the Murry Downs Station, about twenty miles outside of Hay. The owners of the property, Peter and Lyn Murry, were friends of my parents. The homestead was absolutely beautiful. They had a stunning garden shaded by gum trees and wattles. We were married under a trellis laced with purple wisteria. My dress was a simple, white, form-fitting gown with a Queen Ann neckline and a traditional angel-cut veil." Olivia pointed to the photo she held.

"Oh, Olivia, you look stunning."

"I felt like a princess."

"And your prince doesn't look so bad himself."

"I know, he is so handsome. Here, you can look through this stack of the ceremony. You don't need me giving you a play by play. Do you need a refill on your coffee?"

"No, I'm good, thanks."

"Okay, I'll be right back."

Returning from the kitchen, Olivia picked up another stack of photos and handed them to Suzanna. "Here are a few of the reception. I loved that we had one large, long table outside under the stringed lights. It was magical."

"Looks so inviting and casual, I love the setting and the small group, so intimate. I wish I could have been there. I'm sorry I couldn't get the time off."

"I wish you could have, too. I understand, it was pretty short notice."

"I want to get to the best part. How was the honeymoon?"

"Oh my goodness, the honeymoon of a lifetime. We drove to Victoria and spent a week travelling the Great Ocean Road. The rugged Australian coastline was breathtaking, with stunning views of the ocean and lush landscapes. We stopped at various places along the way. We came across an amazing rainforest that we walked into for about two miles, crossed over five creeks. We had to step on large rocks to get to the other side. We came to the most incredible waterfall. The sound of the water cascading over the rocks and the clear pool of water had us hypnotized."

"Looks incredible, I can't believe how clear the water is. And look at all the lush greenery and the ferns, they're so big," said Suzanna.

Reaching for another stack of photos, Olivia explained, "We stayed a few nights in Apollo Bay, it's a little coastal town nestled into the hills beside the ocean. We stayed in a wooden lodge overlooking the town and the ocean. We had a spectacular view. We lay in bed in the morning and could watch the waves roll in onto the smooth, sandy beach. It got a little chilly at night, as it was the beginning of fall. Kev would light a fire in the stone fireplace in the living room. One morning I woke up and the first thing I saw when I opened my eyes was the fire burning in the fireplace. The bright red flames dancing around the wooden logs made me feel so cozy, and the light rain pattering on the roof was soothing. When I rolled over I could see the ocean and the beginnings of first light."

"Sounds heavenly."

"Oh, it was. Later that morning we saw the most beautiful rainbow across the sky. Here, see how the beginning of it is sitting on top of the ocean and the other end is somewhere here in the hills. The colors were so bright and intense. It was slowly moving towards us, followed by the rain. That same day, travelling the road, we saw a total of five rainbows."

"Wow you had a very colorful day," laughed Suzanna.

Laughing, Olivia replied, "Yes we did."

Picking up a stack of photos, Suzanna said, "Oh, and you saw penguins? They're so cute."

"Yes, we stayed one night on Phillip Island and saw the fairy penguins come in from the ocean, cross the beach, waddle into the bush to find their burrows. It's a nightly ritual that many people pay to see. Kev and I sat on the beach waiting for the sun to go down, as they only come out of the ocean when it's dark. We sat for nearly an hour, snuggled in a blanket trying to get warm. It was around fifty degrees and windy. But it was well worth the cold and the wait. They call it the penguin parade, which happens every evening, and it's a completely natural occurrence. The little tiny penguins were so cute waddling in the sand to find their nesting areas to find shelter and food."

"Oh, they are so sweet."

"Here, look at this lighthouse. It's Cape Otway Lighthouse, the second lighthouse to be built in Australia. We were able to walk up the inner winding staircase to the top, where we stepped outside to the walkway. We looked directly down into the swells crashing onto the rocks below. I was a little scared, especially with the wind blowing so hard it was pushing me around."

"It looks amazing. I've never been in a lighthouse before."

"It was an amazing experience. Not sure of when I'd do it again. My fear of heights kicked in that day. I can still remember the tingling I got in my legs as they turned to rubber. Oh, here is the last day of our travels before returning to Hay. These are the Twelve Apostles," Olivia explained as she pointed at the photo. "They are a collection of limestone stacks off the shore of Port Campbell National Park. There were originally twelve, but years of erosion and the ocean water have collapsed some. I think there were nine left when we visited. They are stunningly beautiful with the raging water crashing on them. I'm not sure what was up with the weather that day. It was unseasonably cold. There were gale-force winds that blew the light, misty rain onto our faces that felt like stinging needles. Oh, we were so cold."

"It looks freezing."

"Thank goodness when we arrived back in Hay the weather had warmed up. The remaining days of our honeymoon, we explored Hay again and all the places we used to hang out. Met up with old friends whom we never thought we'd ever see again."

"I'm sure everyone was surprised to see you two again."

"Yes they were. They couldn't believe our story but weren't surprised we were married."

"Olivia, I'm so happy for you. Your wedding looked perfect, and I loved all the places you went. I'm definitely going on the next trip with you."

"You're on."

"When do you come back to work?"

"On Monday. I need the rest of the week to recuperate. There's something about travelling back across the equator that leaves the body exhausted. Feels like I'm in a bit of a fog, like I've got the flu."

"Well, I've got to go. I'll let you get some rest."

"Thanks for coming by."

"I'm happy I did, I enjoyed hearing about your trip." They walked to the front door.

"I'll see you next week," Suzanna said as she waved goodbye and walked out the door.

CHAPTER 16

Sitting at her desk at work, engrossed in a patient's chart, she didn't hear Hazel walk in. "Morning, Olivia."

Startled, Olivia looked up. "Oh, morning, Hazel, you scared me."

"You looked like you were really caught up in what you were reading."

"I am. I have another consult that really has me perplexed."

"I'm sorry, because I have another consult for you."

"Please tell me it's for advice on completing an advance directive?"

"No, it's not, sorry. There is a twenty-two-year-old in Room 5 with a drug overdose. It's bad. The final testing is positive for brain death. The family is going to need your help."

Leaning back in her chair and staring at the ceiling, Olivia replied, "I hate those cases. They are so sad and maddening." She sighed. "Okay, I'll take a look at the chart this afternoon."

"Thanks, I appreciate it. Oh, and how are the newlyweds?"

"Great. Loving married life. We have settled into a routine of work and home."

"What's it been, two months since you got back from Australia?"

"Actually, going on three months. The time has flown; we have been so busy. We are in the early stages of planning to move back home for good."

"That's great for both of you, but you will really be missed here. We will have to have a big going away party for you."

"Maybe just a small gathering to say goodbye, keep it simple."

"We will figure it out, but I've got to run. I need to set up for a cardioversion. I'll talk to you later. I'm really happy for you."

"Thank you. I'll find you later and update you on Room 5."

Kev was at the stove when she walked in from the garage after arriving home from work. Olivia walked up behind him and wrapped her arms around his waist, laying her head on his back. "Long day?" Kev asked as he stirred the soup.

Sighing, she replied, "It was a long, sad day. Sometimes I really hate my job."

"Come on, Liv, couldn't have been that bad. You're helping people get through the worst days of their lives."

"It was that bad. Lost a young man today over something so senseless, his poor parents were inconsolable. The only good that came out of it was they wanted to donate his organs."

"Oh, cripes," Kev said as he turned to face her. "Sorry, that must have been really hard."

"Yeah, it was. I'm going to shower, then I'll be ready to eat. Are you feeling okay? You look pale."

"I'm alright. I'm feeling a little run down, nothing to worry about. Go on and get in the shower, take your time. I'm not really hungry."

CHAPTER 17

Lying together in bed that morning, with her head resting on his chest, his arm around her shoulder, and the other arm loosely around her waist, he said "Liv, we need to talk. You know how I haven't been feeling very well these past few weeks? I went to see Dr. Breland yesterday and it looks like it's back." Inhaling a sharp intake of air, she struggled to rise up on one elbow to look at him. There she could see the dark truth written on his face. Tears sprang to her eyes and began rolling down her cheeks, blurring her vision. "Hey come on, love, it'll be alright. I've beaten it all those times before. Maybe it won't be as bad as last time. I'm a lot stronger now that I have you."

"How can this be happening? Everything in our lives has been going so well."

"I know it's really not fair. Every time I have an exciting event in my life I get sick. For a while there I stopped hoping for anything, until you came along. I remember the first time I got sick was when I graduated from college and had a job offer in Boston. I was so excited to go, then I ended up getting sick. That was when I was first diagnosed. After that I was promoted and was offered a job in England. It was a lifetime opportunity. Then the leukemia came back after being in remission for almost five years. I was devastated. This last time you found me I was preparing to launch my own company in Australia. Again it derailed my life plans. I don't understand this bloody disease. How do go I go for years in remission, then all of a sudden it comes back right out of the blue? Am I cursed or something? Now that we have plans to move back to Hay, it's back again. I just don't understand," he said, close to tears.

Wrapping her arms around him and burying her face in his chest, she attempted to stifle her cries. He held her tightly, feeling overwhelmed, thinking, *Will this be it? Am I gonna come out of this one, or has my luck finally run out?* The thought of not being with Olivia, leaving her alone again, crushed him. He couldn't bear the thought. He started crying, which sent racks of pain through his body. He began shaking so hard he caused her to whimper, as he was holding her like a vice. He suddenly released her, afraid that he had hurt her.

She reached up with both hands touching his cheeks and looked into his eyes. "You'll be okay, I'm here with you. I'll be by your side every step of the way. Our love is not going to end with you dying now. I won't let it. We have just got back to each other. Fate, God, or whatever is directing our destiny, can't tear us apart again. We almost didn't survive the first time."

His tears subsided and he slowed his breathing to catch his breath. "I know, I can't leave you, I won't leave you. But what if this is it?"

She sat up abruptly, so angry she wanted to throw something. "No, this is not it. You will make it, just like you did the other times. Don't you ever doubt or give up on us."

"Liv, I'm not giving up on us, not ever. We have to be realistic. How much more can my body take before it can't take it anymore?"

"Stop," she yelled. Disengaging from his body and flinging herself from the bed, she began to pace. Abruptly stopping, she turned to him, full of anger, "You are not dying on me, you are—" Choking on more tears, she could barely form the word "—not." Getting up from the bed, he walked to her and pulled her into his arms. They held onto each other tightly. Thoughts of losing what they had together spinning wildly through their minds, their hearts felt like they would explode at any moment.

Kev was the first one able to calm his breathing and shake off the nerves that were making him feel lightheaded. "Livie, look at me, come on, Funny Face." Slowly she disengaged herself slightly from his chest and looked up at him. His heart splintered as he could not bear to see the pain in her eyes. Her face was bright red and her eyes were puffy with dark blotches of mascara smeared on her cheeks. Wiping the tears gently away with the pads of his thumb, he did his best to give her a smile, failing miserably. Taking a deep breath to stall for more time, he realized he had to have this particular conversation with her while he could. No matter how painful. "Liv, I'm gonna fight like I've never ever fought in my entire life. I will draw the strength from what I have, to live for you and for me, us. Believe me, Liv, I will fight. But I need you to remember if it doesn't look good and it's weeks of me not getting better, hooked up to those machines and wires."

"No," she cried out. He held her tighter as she tried to pull away.

"Liv, listen to me. If things aren't going to turn out, I want you to follow my wishes and turn everything off. Let me go," he whispered.

Pounding her fists on his chest, she screamed, "No" over and over again. She managed to pull away from him and step back, seething in hurt and anger. Her words hurtled at him at such force he was momentarily stunned. She had never raised her voice at him in a fury of anger. "You are not dying, you are not going to die. How, how could you of all people tell me to pull the plug? That is the most cruel, hurtful thing you have ever said to me," she screamed.

As Olivia ran from the room, she grabbed her robe to cover her shaking, cold, naked body. She didn't hear Kev calling after her. She was hyperventilating, suffocating. She ran through the house, out of the back door, down the stairs, and down the cold grass to the lake. It was a cool March morning and the wind was howling, her long hair picked up by the wind whipping across her burning cheeks, feeling like small knives were cutting her skin, slapping her back to reality. *Stop being so selfish*, she heard a voice inside of her head say. A sharp stab of guilt brought her to her senses. *Oh, fuck*, she thought, *Kev is the one who is sick and I'm acting like a selfish little bitch*, she chided herself. She heard her grandmother's voice from all those years ago when Kev had left. "Life is not easy and it's not always fair. We learn to deal with what comes our way and try our best to get through it. Having those you hold dear to you makes it easier, but losing them makes the next steps harder, not impossible." *I've got to apologize*, she realized and turned and ran back to the house. Calling out his name as she stepped in the back door, she nearly stumbled over him—he was sprawled on the kitchen floor.

CHAPTER 18

Olivia hung up the phone as the intensive care physician came out of Kev's room. She was not familiar with him. He was a moonlighter who picked up an open shift.

"How is he?" she asked.

"He is holding his own for now. We will see how he will do on the high-flow oxygen and antibiotics. If he doesn't respond, then we will have to intubate him."

"If that's what needs to be done, then do it."

"Mrs. Anderson, I have read your husband's chart and his long history. While doing so, I came across his advance directive. We may be at the point where we need to explore this a little further."

"No, we are not," she snapped.

"I know this is very difficult for you, but look at what he has gone through in the past ten years. Do you really want him to suffer again?"

"You know nothing about my husband. There will be no discussion. He is a full code, and that is final," she spat as she turned and walked out of the unit.

Olivia bolted for the door. She had to get out or she would suffocate. She ran out of the intensive care unit, past the guy buffing the floors to the stairwell, stumbled down the three short flights of stairs, and pushed open the door into the basement hallway. She ran as fast as she could down the long hallway, reaching the door to the outside. With both arms outstretched, she pushed at full force and almost fell through the doorway as it swung open, hitting the wall. Regaining her balance, she kept running down toward the lake.

She felt as if the waves of emotion were about to consume her, like her every breath might have been her last. Her anger was fueled like a raging wave crashing against a shore. Just when she began to think her anger would overcome her, she suddenly felt the deepest despair as the receding waves sucked her out deep beneath the undertow, where she felt she would be lost forever. She wanted to give in and sink to the deepest part of the ocean, where no pain existed. As she was about to give up, the strong current forced her to the surface, gulping for air, only to consume her in raging waves of anger again.

As she stood looking over the lake, not seeing the water glistening in the moonlight, she continued to feel the never-ending waves of anger and despair crashing over her. Then suddenly it subsided, leaving her completely exhausted. Numbness spread through her body as she slowly sank to her knees, then sat on her bottom with her legs bent and her arms hugging them. She didn't know how long she sat like this; her brain was too clouded. She slowly unfolded herself and lay down on the soft grass.

As the tears dried on her face, she stared at the cloudless night sky, focusing on the stars. The stars in her vision were not of the American sky. The sky she was gazing at was the sky of her childhood. The Southern Cross, the constellation she loved and grew up under, always feeling safe and secure under their watch. The Southern Cross could tell a thousand stories of their own. She remembered one such story on a warm summer night. Olivia was snuggled deep under the sheet when her dreams were interrupted with the sound of rapping on the window pane. She slipped out of bed and moved toward the window, a little scared of what might be out there. She reluctantly drew back the curtain and pulled up the blind to find Kev on the other side of the window sadly peering in at her. A smile spread across her face. She opened the window slowly to avoid the loud creaks the wooden frame would make if opened too quickly. She did not want to wake her Mum and Dad. "Hey, Kev, what are you doing here? What time is it?" she asked sleepily.

"It's after midnight, I waited 'til Mum and Dad fell asleep before I snuck out. Will you come for a ride with me?"

"Just give me a tick, I'll be right out." She quietly tiptoed to the wardrobe and fished out a pair of shorts and a T-shirt. Quickly changing out of her nightie, she dressed and tied her tennis shoes.

Kev was waiting for her at the window and helped her out as she threw one leg over the windowsill. He grabbed her hand and pulled her toward the backyard to the lane where he had stashed their bikes. "I've got our push bikes over here," he whispered. Once on their bikes, she followed him as they turned onto Water St. and headed toward Parker St. Olivia wasn't sure where they were going; she just followed closely beside him. She didn't rattle on asking stupid questions. Somehow the silence was like a blanket of comfort enveloping them both. They were so used to being with each other they both could sense when the other needed their presence, not their words. They rode the dark, quiet streets of town. Lights were out, people were sleeping, and children were dreaming. As they turned left onto Pine St., a dog started barking.

A few minutes later they reached the Hay War Memorial High School and made their way to the footy oval. Coming to a stop, they got off their bikes and leaned them against the chain link fence. Kev took Olivia's hand and walked her out to the middle of the footy oval. Without a word spoken they lay down side by side, shoulder to shoulder. Gazing at the sky above was breathtaking. There wasn't a cloud to be seen, only endless, rich black darkness with a sea of glistening stars. "Look over there, Liv, see the Southern Cross?"

"Yeah, I see it. I never have to search for it anymore like when I was little. I look up and find it looking back at me," she said wondrously.

"Dad taught me all about the Southern Cross, how if you ever got lost you could find your way back. It's kinda like a compass. It's far out, how it can't be seen if you live in the northern part of the world. Places like Europe and America, they have their own constellations like the Big Dipper. We live down here, and we are the only ones who can see it, like it was put here just for us."

"Tell me more about the stars," she asked eagerly.

"Well Dad told me and his dad told him before that, so I bet his dad did too before that. Anyway, what he said was the Southern Cross constellations are smaller than some other bunch of stars, but it stands out the best 'cause of its shape. People call it a cross, but it really looks more like a kite. There is one star that is the brightest at the foot of the cross; that's the star that points south toward the South Pole."

"Wow, that's really cool. When I look for the Southern Cross, it's in different spots in the sky? I never see it in the same place," said Olivia.

"That's 'cause the earth is always moving, so it depends on what time of the night you are looking at it. So all you have to do is find it in the sky and look for the brightest star."

"What do you do in the daytime if you are lost?"

Kev chuckled. "Yeah, I asked my dad that too. He laughed and told me, 'then you're stuffed, mate, you better carry a bloody compass.'"

Laughing, she said, "Your dad is so funny."

"Yeah, as funny as a three-legged dog."

"Kev, why'd you'd bring me out with you tonight?"

Groaning he said, "I dunno, Liv, but there's something strange going on at home. Ever since that Friday night I stayed at the Pub with you, Mum and Dad are acting really weird. They aren't talking to each other. Dad's not coming home until we are in bed, and he sleeps on the lounge. Mum's being secretive. Hangs up the phone as soon as I walk in the door. I feel really uneasy, like something bad is going to happen. My fourteenth birthday is coming up soon, and Mum won't talk to me about what we could do for it. I really had to get out of the house tonight. I couldn't sleep. For some reason I really needed to see you, Livie."

"Ah, Kev, I'm sure whatever it is that's bothering them will get sorted out."

"I have a terrible feeling in my guts, I can't shake it." Sitting up, he sighed. "I'm sorry I woke you up. Wanna go yabby fishin' in the morning?"

"Yeah, I reckon that will be fun. What time do you want to meet?"

"How 'bout 7:30? Come on, let's head home."

Olivia closed her eyes, reeling from the memory of the last night she saw Kev before he was taken away. He never showed up the next day to go yabby fishing. *Now, all these years later, I have him back and he might die.*

CHAPTER 19

Sitting in the consult room with Dr. Breland and Victoria, Olivia was holding onto her composure by a thread. She had been up for nearly forty-eight hours. Fear, anger, and hope were fueling her on. "He is presenting as he did on his last hospitalization. His white count is very low, he has pneumonia, and is again septic. My recommendation is to proceed with a bone marrow transplant. I have placed him on the donor list. We need to proceed quickly. The sooner he receives the transplant, the better the outcome. Any questions?" Dr. Breland asked in his monotone voice.

"What if he doesn't get the transplant in time?" Victoria asked

"I'm certain his prognosis will be very dire."

Olivia sat in the chair, too numb and exhausted to speak. After finding him unconscious two days ago, she was consumed by guilt for having fought with him. She didn't want their last moment together to be one of anger. *No*, she told herself, *he will be alright. He'll make it through this, he has to.* Dr. Breland stood up, shook Victoria's hand, nodded to Olivia, and left the room, closing the door behind him. Victoria sat in a well-tailored suit more fitting for a boardroom meeting than a meeting about her son. She looked so smug, Olivia felt disgusted being in the same room with her.

"I told you not to get involved with my son. You should have left well enough alone. You thought he was all yours.

Well, now you get what you deserve. I hope his death crushes you," she said.

It took every ounce of strength Olivia had left not to bite back. Instead she planned to play her. When he was sick last year, he was never matched with a donor. Her fear was that he wouldn't again this time. "How's Jimmy?" Olivia asked.

"What do you mean? He is dead."

"I don't believe you. You'd do anything to keep people Kev cares about out of his life. You told him I was dead, you told him Jimmy was dead. That way you have him all to your sick self."

"You are delusional, girl."

"The only one who is delusional is you, in your selfish and heartless mind."

"You bitch, how dare you."

Olivia could see her take the bait; becoming angry was what Olivia wanted Victoria to do. "When Kev gets better, I'm going to tell him what you've done. Do you really think he'd want anything to do with you? He loved Jimmy more than you. Jimmy was a good father. Just think of the time he'd want to spend with him. Probably would want to go live near him."

Hurtling herself up from the chair, Victoria, in near hysterics, yelled "That weak, pathetic, useless husband. Made nothing of himself. The last thing I'll allow is for Kev to go back to live in Australia and rot in Victoria with that son of a bitch. He killed a man. He thought he was so smart, ringing me, thought he had finally found me. What, did he think I was daft? As soon as I heard his voice and saw the call was from Australia with a Melbourne area code, I knew it was him; I hung up and changed my number."

Smiling, Olivia stood up, "Thanks, Vic. I'll be leaving now. It's time I caught up with Jimmy."

Realizing what she had divulged, Victoria lunged toward her but Olivia sidestepped her as the door was opened by Suzanna. "Is everything alright in here? I thought I heard someone yelling."

"It's okay, I was just leaving," said Olivia.

CHAPTER 20

Braking hard as she pulled into the garage, she slammed the car into park, jumped from the driver's seat, and flew through the kitchen door. She threw her bag on the floor, where it slid across and smacked into the pantry, the contents spilling out. She hurried to the phone, and with trembling fingers she dialed the international number. She got a pre-recorded message: "Your call cannot go through. Please check the number and dial again." She repeated the process, only to find she'd been entering the wrong numbers. She slammed the phone into the receiver with a loud cry of frustration.

Scowling at the phone as if it were deliberately betraying her, she took a deep breath. Picking up the phone again, she slowly dialed the ten digit number again. She was rewarded with a ringing sound as the call went through. Drumming her fingers on the kitchen counter, she prayed Kerri would answer the phone. It was three o'clock tomorrow morning in Australia, and knowing what a deep sleeper Kerri was, Olivia was afraid she would not answer.

Relief spread through her as she heard a sleepy voice say, "This better be bloody good." Smiling, Olivia could envision her cousin with a grumpy look on her face, sitting up in bed and pushing her thick red hair away from her eyes.

"Kerri, it's me, Olivia. I've got to talk to you, I need your help."

The sleepiness falling from her voice, Kerri said, "What's wrong, Liv? Is it Kev?"

"Oh, Kerri! We need to find a donor; we are running out of time. It's a long story, but I had it out with Victoria."

"Again?"

"Yeah, I'll tell you about it later. I goaded her into revealing that Kev's dad is alive and several years ago she received a phone call from Australia with Melbourne's area code. She said she answered it and heard a man's voice on the other end. She knew it was Jimmy, and she immediately hung up and never answered the continued calls. She changed her number soon after that."

"What a selfish, bloody bitch," Kerri said. "All along, her son has had the dark stench of death breathing down his neck, and she doesn't get ahold of the one person in the world who may have a chance of saving Kev's friggin' life. Oh, what I wouldn't do to put my hands around that woman's neck and squeeze the life out of her sorry soul."

Exhaling, Olivia said, "I know. I can't believe she could be this selfish and single-minded. She wants to keep her son all to herself, even if it means letting him suffer all the times when he has been so sick. I can't even try to understand her warped mind."

"She doesn't have a friggin' mind in that stupid head of hers. So all we know is Jimmy is alive and he was bloody close in finding her."

"She told me Jimmy was a terrible husband and that he is a murderer."

"Struth," Kerri said, letting out a loud sigh, "That's one cold-hearted bitch. I don't believe Jimmy killed anyone, not the Jimmy we knew as kids. He had a heart of gold."

"Yeah, and her heart is made of stone. I need your help digging around. We have to find him. What if he is a match for Kev for a bone marrow transplant? We have to find him," she said pleadingly.

"Alright, let me grab a pen and paper. I want you to tell me everything you can remember about Jimmy. Hang on a tick while I get up." Olivia stood holding the phone. As she heard Kerri fumble around she heard a loud shatter of glass, then a loud curse, "Shit."

"Are you alright?" Olivia asked.

"Yeah, I'm good, just knocked over the bedside lamp. Didn't like it anyway; was an ugly thing I picked up at the op shop. Alright, I'm in the lounge room. I've got a pen and paper, shoot."

Olivia closed her eyes and strained to bring forth memories of her childhood with Jimmy. She could see him and remember the fine lines etched around his eyes that would crinkle when he smiled, his skin the color of sunburnt leather from hours of being in the warm Australian sun. In those days she was sure not a drop of sunscreen had ever touched his skin. He was tall with broad shoulders and big arms. His hair was almost always covered with a well-worn Akubra, and he had the bluest eyes, mirroring Kev's. His blonde, wavy hair was always a bit messed up from wearing his hat. He and Kev resembled each other so closely. His voice was deep, and his words always held warmth. He was a kind man who loved to make people laugh. He'd never met a stranger; he'd talk to anyone.

"Come on, what are you remembering?" Kerri asked impatiently.

"I'm envisioning him—how he looked, how he sounded."

"Well, that's not much to go on."

"It's a start. You are going to have a description of him. You remember him too, don't you?"

"Yeah, I do. I really liked him. He was always jokin' around. I'm sure I would recognize him if I saw him."

"Are you sure? It's been sixteen years."

"I'm sure he hasn't changed that much, probably looks older. He may have changed his hair or grown a beard, but I'm sure I'd recognize him. Wasn't he close to his mum and dad? I remember him taking off to Narrandera all the time to check on them."

"That's right, he was. I'm not sure if they are even alive now. We should check into it though. It's the only thing we have to go on," Olivia replied hopefully.

"What were their names?"

"Umm, I can see them in my mind. Nice old couple. At least, they looked pretty old to me when I was a kid. They used to visit a lot and come to family barbies. Oh! Their names are right on the tip of my tongue. Oh, come on," she said has she tapped her forehead and squeezed her eyes closed. She suddenly yelled out, "Peter and Betty Thompson! I remember."

"Thank goodness. I thought I was gonna fall asleep just waiting for you to give me a name."

"Ah, very funny. I also remember his grandparents were William and Joan Bainbridge. What do ya think the chances are of him changing his name to William Bainbridge? Would be pretty easy to change dates on a birth certificate, especially back then."

"Good on ya. Now we may have a name to go on. You better be right about that, or we will be on a wild goose chase for nothing."

"Oh, I hope I'm right. His dad may be the only chance Kev has left. We have to find him. I have to at least try and see if he is a match."

Hearing the tears in her voice, Kerri reassuringly said, "Now, don't get your hopes up too high, we have to find him first. I'll do a search online, check out the office of vital records, and check if there is a deed for purchase of any land in his name. I'm flying to Melbourne on Monday for a showing of my newest paintings at the Melbourne Art Gallery. I'll extend my time there a few more days and scout around the area. Jimmy was a mechanic, wasn't he?"

"Yes, a really good one. If he was making a living, I'd bet he is a mechanic somewhere."

"Alright, hang in there. I'll ring you in a few days and keep you updated on what I find. I may as well start now, I'm not gonna be able to go back to sleep now."

"I'm sorry, I just couldn't wait," Olivia said.

CHAPTER 21

Olivia suddenly awoke with fear as she heard the loud piercing of the phone. She feared it was the hospital calling. Her heart was drumming so fast it made her breathing ragged. Quickly picking up the cordless phone, she shouted, "Hello!"

"Hey, take it easy, Liv. It's just me, Kerri."

"Oh, thank God!" Olivia breathed as she slumped back onto the pillows. She squinted at the clock radio, registering the blue digital numbers displaying 4:30 a.m.

"Liv, you there?"

Inhaling deeply, she felt her shattered nerves begin to calm. "Yes, it's just I get so scared when the phone rings. I don't want it to be the hospital, telling me," her voice trailed off.

"Brace yourself, I found him."

Bolting upright, Olivia cried out, "You found him?"

"Is there an echo? I could have swore I just said that."

"Ah, Kerri, you are driving me crazy. Where is he? Did you talk to him? Is he coming?"

"Slow down. No, not quite. I'll fill you in."

On edge, Olivia jumped out of bed and began pacing the room. "Okay, I'm listening."

Kerri began to recite, "After the showing at the art gallery—which went well, by the way—"

Olivia clutched the phone and waved her free hand in the air, thinking, *Come on, come on and get to the point.*

"My online search wasn't very helpful. I couldn't get access to death certificates or property sales. So driving back to the Point from Griffith, I took a detour and headed over to Narrandera. I remember going to Kev's grandparents' house on school holidays with you and Kev. They lived right next door to the Fig Tree Motel on Cadell St. I was taking a chance that maybe his grandparents still lived there. I knew the chances were slim, but I had to try. If they weren't still there, then I thought of the younger couple that lived next door to them; we used to play with their kids. I was thinking if they still lived there they might be able to tell me where they would have moved to. When I got to the house it was as I remembered it. One-story little white house with the white fence out front and the old creaky gate. The huge fig tree is still there, towering over the side of the house. The house had been sold, nice old lady told me they had bought it about sixteen years ago. She didn't know what happened to the owners. She had never met them. The house was vacant when they bought it.

Disappointed, I went next door and was relieved to find that the Carmichaels still lived there. They are much older now, but they remembered us as kids. They told me that Jimmy's dad had died a long time ago, but his mum was still alive. They weren't exactly sure where she moved to. They remembered that Jimmy came and got her one day, left everything there. Some packers came a few days later and cleared everything out. They did get to say goodbye to Betty before she left. She had told them she was moving to Victoria to be closer to her son. For several years they received Christmas cards from her, then they stopped coming. The mention of that really got my attention. I asked if they still had the cards.

Thankfully, Mrs. Carmichael is a packrat and keeps everything she gets. She brought out a shoebox full of cards. We sat at the kitchen table and looked through the entire box. Tucked in the very back was a Christmas card still in the envelope. What were the chances of that happening? I couldn't believe it. It had the return address for a retirement home in Ballarat."

"Oh my god, Kerri, I can't believe it. She's alive?"

"Hang on, let me keep going, don't get ahead of me. At first I wasn't too sure if she was still alive; the postage mark on the last Christmas card was dated 1999. So when I got home I rang the retirement home and asked for Betty Thompson. They didn't have anyone there with that name. I started askin' questions, but they wouldn't give me any more info. Something about privacy and shit. So I started thinkin', if Jimmy wanted to go into hiding and he changed his name then it would make sense to change his Mum's name too.

"Instead of ringing the home again I thought I'd just go there myself. I drove east for about two hours out of Melbourne to Ballarat. It was a nice drive, the bush is so pretty this time of year. I found the retirement home on the west side of town. It looked real nice on the outside, a wide verandah with rocking chairs. The place was surrounded by big red gum, wattles, and eucalyptus trees. The gardens were beautiful, with hundreds of native wildflowers and rosebushes. I could tell they kept the place up. When I went inside it didn't have the smelly stink of old people. You know how some places try to hide the stench of urine with loads of air freshener and cleaning chemicals? No matter how much they use them, the ammonia smell of old people's piss still hits you in the face."

On the other end of the line, Olivia was biting her lip so she didn't say out loud, *Come on, Kerri, I don't need a friggin' description of the place.* Not having a clue to her impatience, Kerri continued, "I found the receptionist desk. There was a young little tart with loads of make-up, gossiping on the phone. I'm sure it was a personal call. I had to wave at her to get her attention. She finally hung up the phone and I told her I was here to visit Joan Bainbridge. She gave me a surprised look. She asked how I knew Mrs. Bainbridge, not that it was any of her business. I told her she was an old neighbor of mine when I was a kid. She told me she doesn't get many visitors, just an old friend of the family visits every Sunday. I acted like I knew who she was talking about: a tall older bloke, blonde and grey hair with a beard? She asked me how I knew Bill. Told her he was an old neighbor too."

"Wow! That was really tricky of you. You got her to confirm that it's Jimmy, from the sounds of it, and now we know he has a beard and visits every Sunday. It's got to be him."

"Yeah, I thought so myself, she finally told me she was in Room 220. I hurried off, as I didn't want the nosey twit asking me any more questions. I found the stairs and walked to the end of the hall.

"I found Joan sitting by the window reading a book. I told her who I was and she just stared at me blankly. She had smoky, clouded, pale blue eyes and a million wrinkles deeply lining her face. Her short, curly hair had a blue tinge to it. I didn't think old ladies still colored their hair that light blue anymore like they did when we were kids. She mumbled, 'Gotta get the sheep to the shearing shed today.' I ignored her attempt at being batty. I told her about Kev and how sick he was, how I needed to find Jimmy to help Kev. The old bat wasn't foolin' me. I was watching her reaction and could see her pupils widen just a bit and her gnarled up, crooked fingers were squeezing the book she was holding so tight her knuckles turned white. I told her to cut the bull. Even though she looked older than dirt, I could tell she understood what I was talking about. What eighty-year-old lady could read *The Thorn Birds*? That's an Aussie classic, that's not an easy read. She didn't say a word, just kept staring out the window.

"I walked over to her dressing table and noticed a jar of sherbet lemon drops. I remember you telling me about those. How they were her favorite lollie that made her smell like lemons. I asked her if Jimmy brought her these. No response from her. She was sitting so rigid, I thought if I tapped her on the shoulder she would shatter. I got tired of the charade and finally sat on the windowsill so she would have to look at me. I told her I wasn't there to get Jimmy in trouble, I just needed to talk to him and let him know about Kev. Then I told her about you, Liv, how you and Kev found each other and were married. That was what finally cracked her shell.

"She was really shaken up and said, 'Kev and Liv, those sweet kids. I knew they would be together someday. They had such a special bond.' She was crying. I felt like such a bitch goin' at her so strong, but I guess it did the trick. Got her to open up; she told me that Jimmy came for her after his dad died and moved her down here. He had changed her name to her mother's name to keep her safe. He wasn't so sure if any of the boys back in Hay would be after him, so he played it safe. I asked why they would be after him, and I told her we knew as kids something bad had happened but no one would tell us why. She said, 'That wife of his killed her lover and blamed it on Jimmy. She left town and left him to take the rap—oh, those were some terrible days.'"

"Oh, that's horrible," Olivia said. "Now it all makes sense why she left town, but it doesn't explain why Kev never contacted me."

Kerri interrupted; she didn't want Olivia to go down that road again right now. "You were right, he changed his name to William 'Bill' Bainbridge, just like his poppy."

"She told me he is a mechanic on one of the big sheep stations around here. He keeps low and out of sight, working on the property fixing all the farm machinery. He lives in a bungalow on the property. He comes to town every Sunday for supplies and to visit his mum. After the initial shock of hearing about Kev, she got pretty riled up. She was ravin' mad at Victoria, said a few choice swear words and a thing or two about what she'd like to do to her. She never liked that selfish bitch, said she knew she put on a front around other people, but saw right through it. She told me that no one has ever come looking for her or Jimmy. The fact that we found them was a sign that he needed to come out of hiding and go help his son. He would want to, as he has never been the same without Kev. He walks around like a piece of himself is missing."

Finding her voice, Olivia said sadly, "I know exactly how he feels. I lived like that for years until I found Kev."

"It's getting late here, I'm gonna go to the pub for some tea and get to bed early. I'm driving out to the McPhillips sheep station early tomorrow morning. I'm going to find Jimmy and let him know he is finally gonna see his son. Hopefully I'll have him on the next plane to you. Look, I'll ring you tomorrow and let you know how it goes."

Feeling the first rays of hope seep into her body, Olivia said optimistically, "He'll come, I know he will. He has to be a match. He holds the last thread of hope to save Kev. Oh, thank you for all of your help."

"Don't thank me just yet. I'll ring you tomorrow. Say g'day to Kev for me. See ya," Kerri said, and she hung up the phone.

CHAPTER 22

Checking the map one final time, Kerri tossed it unfolded onto the passenger seat. She put the rented Land Rover into gear and pulled out of the pub's car park. She estimated it would take her about an hour to drive to the McPhillips Station, since she really wasn't sure where she was going. Heading South on the Midland Highway on the outskirts of Ballarat, the traffic had thinned and the unbridled beauty of the bush came into focus. The strain of the past several days began to fall away with each kilometer she drove. Beginning to relax, her thoughts turned toward Kev's dad. How was he going to react to seeing her after all these years? Being accused of a crime he didn't commit, how would that have changed him? Question after unanswered question streamed through her mind. Poor Jimmy: his life destroyed and his only son lost. She wasn't sure how he felt about Victoria, that bloody bitch. *If I were him*, she thought, *I'd knock her bloody block off and shove her in the river.*

About forty-five minutes down the road, Kerri pulled into a rundown service station for petrol. After she put sixty bucks in the tank, she thought she might get something to eat. The vegemite and toast she'd had this morning was not enough. She walked over to the small café that was advertising "The Best Meat Pies." A large, weathered, wooden black and red sign hung over the café entrance, declaring she had arrived at Frank & Flo's. Bells tinkled and chimed as she opened the wooden screen door. Removing her sunglasses, she allowed a minute for her eyes to adjust to the dimmer lighting. She saw that the café was almost empty save for a young couple in a booth in the back of the room. She walked over to the counter and was greeted by a short, bald, heavyset man somewhere in his sixties. His face was round with several double chins, making her think that he probably enjoyed eating the food as much as serving it.

As she approached the counter and took a seat, his face broke into a big toothy smile that made her feel welcome. "G'day love, the name's Frank."

"Hi, I'm Kerri."

"What can I get ya, you hungry?"

"Yeah, my stomach's been growling the past twenty Ks. Says out front you have the best meat pies."

"Betcha we do. The missus makes them fresh evra mornin'. We got plain, steak 'n mushroom, steak 'n kidney, or lamb 'n onion."

"Plain for me, and a coke please."

"Righto, I'll go in back and pop one in the oven. Be just a tick."

Frank headed through the swinging double doors, calling out to his wife, "Flo, we got a customer." As she waited for her pie she looked around the café. It looked like it had been here for many years, with traditional woodwork, crown molding, tin ceiling tiles, and scuffed up wooden floor boards that lent it character. The tables and chairs were the old style chrome metal she remembered as a kid. She was surprised to notice how spotlessly clean it was for an older establishment. She pulled the map out of her bag and spread it over the counter. She tried to estimate how much further she had to go and in what direction to find the McPhillips Station. She was starting to get worried, as the smaller roads were probably not listed on the map.

She looked up as Frank, who set down her meat pie and coke next to her. She pushed the map to the side and slid the plate closer. "Ta."

"That's alright, love. Where you headed to?" he asked curiously as he handed her a bottle of tomato sauce. In between bites, she explained she was looking for the McPhillips Sheep Station. "What business you have with them?" he asked with suspicion.

Hiding her surprise, she responded casually, "I'm lookin' for an old friend of the family, we lost track a few years back."

"Well I know all the locals around here. Who exactly you looking for?"

She took another bite of the pie to give her time to decide if she should tell him or not. Gone was the friendly bloke she had just met. He was glaring at her with a cautionary look. She couldn't figure out if he was warning her or protecting someone. She took her chances and said, "Billy Bainbridge, or as I know him, Jimmy."

He leaned in close to her, placing his chubby hands on either side of her plate. Looking her right in the eye, he said, "Neva heard of him. So if I were you I wouldn't waste your time drivin' out there."

"I spoke to Joan, his mum. You don't need to protect him."

"Look, if you were sent here by that guy's family, I'm tellin' you he didn't do it. You leave him alone, he's a good bloke, done nothin' wrong, poor bloke got framed for a murder he didn't do."

Swallowing the last bit of pie that had gone dry in her mouth, she said, "I know he was set up. I'm here about his son."

Stepping back in surprise, Frank could barely compose himself. "Struth! His boy? Why, he's been gone for years. His mother took off with him, never seen or heard of them since. Broke Jimmy's heart, never been the same."

"I've been searching for Jimmy for weeks. I have to talk to him," Kerri said. Then she paused before saying, "I know where his son is."

Reaching for a serviette off the counter and a pen from his apron, he pushed her map aside, telling her the bloody thing wouldn't have done her any good; she would have ended up in Timbuktu. Handing her the directions, he said, "Now get a move on."

Startled, Kerri said, "Alright, let me pay for you for the food and I'll be on my way."

"No, it's on the house. Get going, he has been waitin' long enough," he said as he haphazardly folded the map and shoved it into her hands.

Kerri picked up her bag and headed for the door. She was about to go through the door when she turned back and yelled out, "Thanks, Frank, you're right. You do have the best meat pies." Smiling, she got into the Land Rover and turned left onto the Midland Highway.

She followed Frank's directions as best she could, though his handwriting was like chicken scratch. She made the final turn onto a narrow, rutted dirt road, flanked by nothing but wild bushes and brown grass. She had to slow to stop the dry red dust from spinning up and masking her vision through the windows. Rounding a bend, she came to a long fence that appeared to go on for miles. She stopped at a gate that had a small sign posted, "McPhillips Sheep Station." She put the vehicle in gear, unfastened her seat belt, and got out. She was happy she had worn her favorite Levis and boots, as the dust was already clinging to her feet and legs. She unlocked the gate, walked back to the rover, and drove through, then got back out to re-lock the gate. Having lived in the bush all these years, she knew the unwritten rule that you always close the gates. No one wanted to be responsible for losing an entire herd of sheep. She hoped there weren't too many more to pass through. *Wishful thinking*, she thought. There would be several more from the looks of how big the property was. Acres and acres of paddocks were fenced off in divided sections.

Closing the fourth gate, she could see a circle of trees in the distance. Likely the house and the outbuildings. She drove beneath a tall iron archway displaying an outline of a Merino and the name McPhillips. Seeing the road split up ahead, the right appeared to lead to a house, the left to the outbuildings. As she drove toward the buildings, she had a better view of the house and could see how beautiful it was. It was a traditional homestead with a wraparound verandah, congregated tin roof, and a beautiful garden. The wattle trees were bright yellow, and there was a sea of roses around the verandah. For a moment she wished she could sit on the wide verandah and have a cuppa to wash down the dust in her mouth.

She pulled up alongside a large metal building and got out of the Rover. Feeling a little nervous, she brushed the dust off and headed for the door. Scanning the buildings, she saw all kinds of farm equipment in some state of disassembly and in the rear of the building an auto bay. She slowly walked toward the bay, where she saw a tractor with the hood up. Looking around, she called, "Hello, hello, is anyone around?" She was met with silence.

She sidestepped some tools and leaned down to peer under the tractor, but there was no one there. Standing back up, she heard a voice whisper, "Kerri."

Startled, she spun around. There stood a man in dirty jeans and a sweat-stained blue work shirt with splotches of black oil on the fabric. The words didn't come, as she was too stunned to see the man who vaguely resembled Jimmy. Underneath the fading blond hair mixed with grey, his blue eyes had dulled as if the light had gone out of him, and his shoulders were slumped as if in defeat. She pushed back the tears that were threatening to fall. She had heard of a broken heart but had never actually seen one. She could see this man's broken heart clearly etched in his face. "Jimmy," is all she could say. For once, words had failed her.

He took two strides toward her and embraced her in a comforting hug. He released her, and she heard the faint echo of the happy Jimmy she knew long ago. "Hey, what's with the waterworks? Where's the little toughie I used to know?"

Smiling, she said, "I'm still here. It's just that I never thought I'd see you again. I've been looking so hard, I can't believe I actually found you." She suddenly stopped, and a look of confusion replaced her smile. "Hang on, how'd you know that was me? You said my name, my back was towards you?"

Grinning Jimmy said, "I'd know that wild head of red hair anywhere, plus Frank rang me."

"Oh, that sneaky old codger," Kerri smiled

Quickly dawning on her and apprehension sinking in, she said, "Did he say why I was coming?"

"Nah, he didn't. Just something about 'you're gonna be alright, mate.' What's he goin' on about?"

"Is there somewhere we could go to sit and talk?"

CHAPTER 23

Olivia sat next to Kev's bed with her left hand snugly holding his. His eyes were closed, his chest moving rhythmically in sync with the ventilator. He had had an uneventful night, becoming slightly agitated when the nurses turned him every two hours and had to suction the secretions from the endotracheal tube. He didn't require much sedation. As soon as he was left alone, he would settle into a deep sleep. His body was just too weak to battle against the nurses' care or the multitudes of medical equipment invading his body.

She had barely slept that night. Every time she felt her body succumb to sleep, she would jerk herself awake, first checking Kev, then the numbers and waves colorfully lighting the monitor. Her eyes first sought the green wave and the number that followed indicating his heart rate. She was relieved to see that he wasn't tachycardic, his heart rate was steady in the 80s to 90s, in a normal sinus rhythm. Then she would scan the purple numbers indicating his blood pressure, which was on the low side at 100/60. The low dose of Levophed was maintaining his blood pressure to keep his organs perfused with blood.

Assured that he was stable, Olivia checked her mobile phone for a missed call. Silly, she thought, she wouldn't have missed a call, as she had stared at it all night willing it to ring. She was anxious to hear from Kerri. She had to know if she had found Jimmy, and most importantly if he would come.

Of course he would. His life had turned into a horror story: framed for murder, losing his life, and being betrayed by a very cruel and selfish woman. As sure as she knew her next heartbeat would come, she knew he would be here.

It was after 6:00 a.m. Olivia stared out of the window overlooking the lake. The sun coming up over the water captured her attention. She never tired of looking at the wonder of beauty before her. The first rays of sunlight emerged, spilling a faint glow of pink light across the water. The lake was coming to life, as if just waking up. The gentle wind made the water ripple, capturing it and sending it into a slow dance. She took in the tranquility of the water playing with the light and she felt peacefulness settle over her. It felt as if someone was placing a light blanket around her shoulder.

The sudden ringing of the phone startled her out of the place she had been. Quickly pulling her hand from Kev's, she grabbed the phone and only succeeded in dropping it into her lap. Her hand had been in his most of the night. Shaking her hand to get the feeling back, she picked the phone up with her right hand, flipped it open, and saw the caller ID read an international number. With shaking fingers she pressed the button to accept the call.

"Kerri," she cried out. The comforting peace she had felt only moments ago were stripped away and were replaced with the all too familiar claws of anxiety and fear.

"Liv, I can't hear you, you are breaking up."

Nearly shouting, she said, "Hang on, Kerri, I'll ring you back on a landline."

She quickly disconnected the call and ran from the room, briefly stopping to pump sanitizer on her hands, flinging gel in her wake as she flew from the unit. Reaching her office and closing the door, she flung herself into the chair and snatched the phone, punching in the numbers for Kerri. She finally took a breath as she heard the call connect.

"Hey, that didn't take ya long."

"I've been a jumbled up set of nerves waiting for you to ring. Tell me, tell me, did you find him?"

"Yeah, of course I did. When I found him he looked like a dead man inside, but now that he knows where Kev is—well, it's a miracle. It's like a light has been switched on," Kerri explained.

"Is he coming?" she asked, holding her breath.

"Of course he is. We are booked into a hotel right near the airport. Our flight leaves in the morning at seven thirty."

"You're coming too?" she yelled in excitement.

"Not gonna let you take all the credit. I wanna be there when Kev wakes up," she said, becoming serious. "Hey, Cuz, don't get your hopes up too high, we don't know if he'll even be a match. I don't want you to be crushed again."

Olivia whipped out with conviction in her voice, "He will. He has to be a match. If there's a God in this world, He won't allow more hurt in my life. For Christ's sake, I have lost my parents and grandparents, each one taking a piece of me with them. If I lose Kev, there will be nothing left of me. I'll be destroyed."

Swallowing a lump that had formed in her throat, Kerri whispered, "I know, Liv, I know."

Pushing through the dark cloud of fear that was always choking her, she asked, "Tell me how it went with Jimmy. I want to know."

"When I first saw him, I was shattered to see the loving, lively Jimmy we knew as kids barely a remnant of himself. He looked like a lost soul, no life in his eyes, and clearly etched on his face was the pain of his broken heart. I have never seen a person who looked so broken. I told him what I saw in him. He admitted that's the way he felt, and he would have given up long ago. The only thing that kept him tethered to this world was his hope in finding his boy one day. He had tried to find him for years. He had hired an investigator, put ads in the papers, scanned thousands of websites and chat rooms. Years ago he thought he had found her. He would randomly ring phone numbers of women with the name Victoria. A woman answered, and it had sounded like her voice, but she hung up before he could talk to her. He tried ringing the number again, but it was disconnected. He prayed and believed that before he died, he would see him again.

"I wish you could have seen the look on his face when I told him where Kev was and has been all these years. He was stunned. First in total disbelief, then I saw the realization hit him. He bent over with his elbows on his knees, his face in his hands as he cried. In his cries I could hear the years of pain, the agony, the loneliness, and finally I heard cries of joy and hope. Couldn't help myself, I gotta a little choked up too. I had never seen a person with so much pent-up emotion finally let it go. When he was able to get himself together, he grabbed me in a tight bear hug, almost knocking the wind out of me. Then all of a sudden he was peppering me with questions. Geez, he was almost as annoying as you. He calmed down enough for me to tell him about you. Oh, was he happy, he couldn't stop smiling, especially when I told him that you two were married. He yelled out, 'You little ripper.' It was funny; no one ever says that anymore. Reminded me of when we were kids. I told him about your lives, the crazy way you found each other and how in love you are. I'm sure his face hurt, 'cause I betcha a smile hasn't been on his face since the day the bloody bitch stole Kev."

Olivia quickly interrupted, for if she didn't, she knew Kerri would go on a tirade about Victoria and what she would do to her. "Did you tell him about Kev and the leukemia?"

Calming down, Kerri continued, "Yeah I did. Hated to, though, he finally felt some happiness and I didn't want to take it away so soon. He took the news well. He said that they'd deal with that when he got there. Together they would fight it. He had an air of confidence. He told me 'No bloody cancer is taking my son. We've got a lot of years to catch up on.' Then all of a sudden, he was a man on a mission. He pulled me by the hand off of the bench we had been sitting on and took off in a full sprint. He dashed into his bungalow, changed clothes, and threw a bunch of clothes in a suitcase in a few seconds flat. He looked at me as if asking, 'what are you waiting for, let's go.' Before we left the station we left word at the house to let Duncan McPhillip know where he was off to. I asked him if we should hang around and talk to the boss, I didn't want him to get sacked. He laughed at me and told me not to worry. Him and Duncan were old mates from when they were kids, so was Frank from the café, been mates for years. They had helped him out when he was released from jail, gave him a job on the station, and helped him keep a low profile. They'd be happy to hear the news.

"On the drive back to Melbourne, I filled him on the rest of how we tracked him down. I answered all the thousands of questions he kept peppering at me. We had tea in the pub's restaurant. After we ate we went to the bar for a few rum and Cokes. Jimmy's not much of a drinker these days, but he seemed like he needed one tonight. Hopefully calmed him down a bit so he can get some sleep tonight." Fighting back a yawn, Kerri said, "I'm buggered, I'm gonna get in the shower and hit the sack. I'll ring you in the morning before we fly out."

With excitement tingling through her body, Olivia said, "Thank you. I couldn't have done this without you. You found him!"

Before she could go on, Kerri replied, "That's what family is for. 'Night."

CHAPTER 24

Olivia had been waiting at the airport terminal for over half an hour for their flight to arrive. She was so excited to be finally seeing Jimmy and Kerri again. She couldn't sit still. Praying he would be a match for Kev, she almost missed the announcement that Flight 4711 had arrived at Gate 14 from Los Angeles. She walked over to the boarding gate, joining a group of people waiting for the arrivals. Passengers began disembarking and walking past her. She stood on tiptoes looking for them. They must have been at the very back of the plane, as the line of passengers began to thin.

She saw Jimmy first because he was so tall and was wearing an Aussie Akubra on his head like he always did. Beside him was Kerri: 5' 5", stylish, shoulder-length hair that was the most shining, beautiful shade of red. Brown eyes and ivory skin with a splash of freckles across her face. As they came closer, she was surprised to see how much Kev looked like his father compared to when he was a boy. He had aged well, except for the worry lines that creased his face. He came lumbering up to her. "G'day, Liv, you haven't changed a bit," he said as he picked her up in a huge, warm hug. "Ah, I've missed you, kiddo." Back on her feet, she smiled, grateful that he was alive and actually here. She hadn't realized how much she had missed him.

"Come here, Cuz." Kerri embraced her in a tight hug. "It's finally good to see ya, bossing me around from halfway across the world. You owe me one," she said, laughing.

"I owe you the world, thank you. I'm so happy you are both here."

"Come on, this is enough of a family reunion. Take me to Kev, I've waited long enough to see my boy."

"Yes, you have."

The drive from the airport to the hospital went quickly as they talked about everything that had happened and how unbelievable it was. Arriving at the hospital, Olivia led them to Kev's ICU room. Pushing the door open, she allowed Jimmy then Kerri to walk in before her. They both walked up to the head of the bed.

Jimmy let out a cry, "Oh, Kev," and began to sob uncontrollably. Kerri stood beside him with tears falling down her cheeks. She turned and left the room, giving them some privacy.

CHAPTER 25

Walking out to the patio with two iced teas and placing one in front of Jimmy, Olivia took a seat. "What in the hell is this, Olivia? You've ruined a perfectly good cuppa by putting ice in it. Don't you remember us Aussies drink our tea hot?" he said.

Smiling, she replied, "I know. I thought it was a bit strange too at first. When I first arrived here, I couldn't go anywhere without seeing people drinking their tea with ice in it. I finally gave in and tried it. I was surprised I liked it. Go on, try it."

Slowly picking up the glass, he took a sip. "Mmm." He nodded. "Okay, not too bad, I reckon. I s'pose I could get used to this on a hot day, now and again."

"Do you still drink that instant coffee at home? I remember everyone drinking it when I was a kid."

"Sure do, Liv. International Roast, with two sugars and milk. Best darn cuppa, beats those fu-fu coffees they sell now."

Her tone became serious as she looked at him and asked, "Jimmy, I need to know what happened back then, when you were accused of murder."

His face jerked toward her, his smile vanishing. He glared at her.

Startled, she could see the anger in his eyes. Reaching for his hand she begged, "Please, I have to know. I need to know why our lives were torn apart for all these years. We'll never get them back. I have to know."

His eyes softened, but his voice had not. Speaking like he had swallowed something awful, he said, "Liv, you know Victoria set me up for that bloke's murder. You don't need to know more than that."

"I do. I need to know to what lengths she went to and what she's capable of." Her voice rose. "She got you out of the way. What makes you think she won't get rid of me?"

Stunned, Jimmy sat up straighter and leaned toward her, "What! Has she threatened you?"

"No, it's not an exact thing. It's just a feeling I get. When Kev and I first got together after he went into remission, she did everything in her power to prevent us from being together. Finally, Kev had to have it out with her and threatened to leave the country with me. That seemed to work. I suppose she couldn't live without him near her so she compromised and put up with me. She was frigidly nice to me when Kev was around. On the rare occasion I was alone with her, she would turn to pure ice and make sly insinuations that closely resembled threats."

"What do you mean, threats?" Jimmy exclaimed, becoming alarmed.

The wind began to pick up as if sensing her turmoil. Brushing her hair away from her face, she explained, "There was one time that particularly stood out. Kev had gone to get the car because it was snowing, leaving Victoria and me in the restaurant's lobby. She glared at me with pure hatred, and I swear her eyes turned a sinister black. I remember so clearly how menacing her voice sounded as she flatly told me, 'So you think you've won? Well, it's not over yet. I'm in charge of his destiny, not you. You are nothing. Just remember I always get what I want.'

"I was too stunned to reply. By then Kev had pulled up with the car. I never told him what she had said. He knew how his mother felt about us being together. We rarely talked about it, as we were not going to have her interfere with our relationship. He was resigned to the fact there was nothing he could do. We weren't surprised when she went into a rage when we told her we were getting married. She badgered Kev constantly to leave me, driving him away from her. We had to secretly leave the country earlier this year and were married in Australia. There is no telling what she would have done if we had married here."

"Ahh, bloody hell, Liv." He groaned as he covered his face with his palms then began rubbing his temples. Inhaling deeply, he looked out toward the water. He didn't seem to notice the wind blowing leaves across the lake and water bouncing along the surface. He was not seeing the present, he was brought back to that fatal night: December 28th, 1976. Olivia's head quickly moved in surprise to look at him because his voice had changed to a much younger Jimmy. She listened to his trancelike recitation of that horrible night.

"I'd just gotten home around half past eight that night. I had worked late at the garage. Vic was gone as she usually was on Friday nights. Kev was with you at the pub. I'd just walked in the house, turning lights on, and was about to take my work boots off when the phone rang. I headed to the front foyer to the phone stand and picked up on the fifth ring. It was Vic, she was screamin' at me to help her. I told her to calm down. I couldn't make out what she was goin' on about. She told me there was an accident and I had to get out to a cabin off Maude road. I knew where she was talkin' about, used to go fishin' near there with me mates. I asked what kinda accident, and she screamed at me to bloody well get here, then she hung up.

"It didn't take me long to get there, 'cause I drove like a bat outta hell. I remember it was strange when I pulled up in front of the cabin. Vic was sittin' on the front steps, calm as a nun in church. I didn't notice blood splattered on her 'til I had jumped out of the ute and ran over to her. At first I thought she was hurt and I needed to get her to the hospital. I knelt down in front of her, I was so scared. As I went to touch her face to figure out where all the blood was coming from, she slapped my hand, yelling that I was an idiot. It wasn't her blood. I reeled back on my knees; my mind was jumbled up and my heart was racing. She calmly and eerily said, 'Over there. He is the one that had an accident.'

"I felt a sense of evil radiating from her. Her pupils were dilated and her eyes were like shiny black stones. I got up and walked over to the car. As I got closer I could smell a strong, coppery odor that made me want to throw my guts up. Then I saw him layin' face down in a massive pool of blood with his brains hangin' out of the huge crack in his head. Poor bloke never knew what hit him.

"I must've been in shock 'cause I didn't hear her come up behind me until she was a few yards away. I have never yelled as loud as I did that night. I strode over to her and grabbed her by the arms and shook her so hard as I shouted, 'What the fuckin hell have you done?' She told me to stop, I was hurtin' her. I had stepped back stunned. I'd never laid my hands on a woman like that before. I was clouded in shock, I couldn't think. She wrapped her arms around me and made noises like she was cryin'. She begged me to help her, she couldn't go to jail. Tellin' me she would die without Kev and me. She told me the bloke was tryin' to hurt her because she wanted to break it off with him. She panicked, grabbed the axe, and split his head wide open.

"I felt like I was in a fog following her instructions. We put him in the boot of his car. I drove a few miles down the road and crashed the car into a tree. I put him in the front seat and poured kerosene over the car and set it on fire. We were far enough away from town it'd be a few days before he would be found. When we got home I took the bloody axe out of the back of the ute. I had planned on burnin' the handle and buryin' the axe head in the bush. Vic told me it was too late to start a fire, so I put the axe in the shed under the tall tool box. After she had showered she came out to the lounge room. I was sittin' in the dark drinkin' a stubby. I couldn't get that bloke's cracked skull out of my head or wrap my mind around how she could've done that. What kind of monster was I married to? She turned on the light and asked me what I was doin'. I yelled, 'Christ, woman, what have you done? You just killed a man, he had a wife and kids.' I was so angry she had brought me in on this. I told her we were gonna burn in hell. She stood there starin' at me with a hint of a smile and those dark black eyes boring into me. It was scary to see her eyes change so dramatically from her usual dark brown.

"She walked over to where I sat and looked down at me. Her voice, I'll never forget the menacing tone as she told me to be a man and stop my whingin'. 'He got what he deserved.' She warned me not to say a word or I'd get what I deserved. She walked away toward the bedroom, stopped, turned to me and sweetly said, 'It's alright, Jimmy, things are going to change.' I slept in Kev's room that night, as I couldn't stand to be near her. Frankly, she scared the hell out of me. I kept replayin' what she had said, 'things are going to change.' What in the bloody hell did that mean?

"Well I found out a few days later when I got home from work. Her car was gone and so were all of her and Kev's things. She left me a nasty note sayin' she and Kev were gone forever. That she hated that I couldn't provide better for her. She was startin' over. I'd never see them again. She'd made sure of it. Then it struck me like a hammer. I dropped the note and ran out to the shed. The axe was gone.

"She had planted the axe outside the cabin. It had my prints on it. I was arrested and put in jail until my trial came three months later. By the time it came up on the docket, the evidence had all gone missin'. They couldn't take me to trial without the axe and the fingerprints. I think your dad had something to do with it. He knew well enough that I'm not a murderer. I don't know how, I'm just grateful he did. I left Hay as soon as I was released. My business had been burnt down, my home vandalized. It wasn't safe for me to stay. The bloke she murdered, his family had a lot of power and could get whatever they wanted done. It was safer to leave, change my name, and become invisible.

"There you have it. Victoria is an incredibly evil woman. So yeah, you have every right to be afraid of her. She will do anything to get her own way. Thinkin' back over that night, she didn't shed one tear over what she had done. No remorse at all."

He looked over at Olivia, who had tears welling in her eyes. He reached for her hand and squeezed, "It's alright, Liv, it worked out. I'm here now, and that's all that matters."

Sniffling, she replied, "Look at what she has done. It has affected us all. How can you be so calm? Don't you want to get revenge? Have her put away for murder?"

"It's too late. I will square it off with her at some point, but right now I can only focus on Kev. He is all that has kept me goin' all these years."

Wiping her eyes, Olivia asked anxiously, "If she's capable of anything, then why hasn't she got rid of me?"

Hesitantly he replied, "I've been wonderin' that myself."

CHAPTER 26

Olivia was in her office taking notes for the upcoming family conference for an eighty-two-year-old man who'd suffered cardiac arrest a week ago. The family was struggling with the decision to end life support. Two EEGs had come back negative for functional brain activity. He didn't have an advance directive documenting his wishes. In the past he had told his children he wouldn't want to be kept alive by machines if he couldn't get well. His wife had passed and the only thing he looked forward to was fishing. If he couldn't do that then let him go.

The ringing of the phone interrupted her thoughts as she reached for the receiver and placed the pen on her desk. "Hello this is Olivia with Palliative Care, how can I help you?"

"Hi, this is Helen at the front desk. There's someone here to see you."

"I don't have any appointments scheduled today," replied Olivia.

"No, she said she didn't have one, but she says it's very important that she speaks with you." Glancing at her calendar, she saw her schedule was clear for the next few hours. She had most of her notes completed for the family meeting at two o'clock. "Okay, Helen, tell her I'll be down. Have her wait in the lobby, please."

As she was stepping off the elevator, she almost collided with a lab cart. "Oh Lynn, you're in a rush."

"Hi, sorry. I've got to hurry. I have stat labs up on the floor." Sidestepping the cart, Olivia replied, "It's okay, hope your day slows down a bit." She heard a muffled "Thanks" as the elevator doors began to close.

Turning into the main hallway that led to the lobby, she could see a tall woman standing by the window. As she approached she could see the woman had short blond hair in a stylish bob. Olivia estimated she was 5' 8". She was dressed in low heels and a nicely-fitted pant suit. The woman turned to face Olivia just as she approached. She appeared to be in her late thirties, green eyes beside high cheek bones. Smiling, Olivia introduced herself as she held out her hand. The woman smiled weakly and shook her hand with a strong grip. "Hello, I'm Meredith Stevens."

"It's nice to meet you. How can I help you?"

Looking around, Meredith asked, "Is there somewhere we could talk privately? It's a personal matter that involves Kev."

Startled, Olivia stared at the woman, briefly at a loss for words. Instantly on guard, Olivia thought, *What does this woman know about Kev?*

Seeing Olivia's reaction, Meredith hurriedly explained, "I'm sorry I've surprised you. I knew Kev growing up. He was my stepbrother."

With a look of confusion, Olivia said, "I don't understand, Kev never mentioned he had a stepsister."

"I'm not surprised he never mentioned me. The last time we saw each other we didn't part on good terms."

"I'm sorry, Ms. Stevens, I don't understand what this is about?"

"Call me Meredith. I'll explain, but not here." Knowing they would be interrupted in her office, Olivia suggested they walk down to the lake. Meredith nodded and followed her out the front doors and down the sidewalk that led to the lake. They didn't speak until they had reached a bench under the trees beside the water. It was overcast with a gentle, cool breeze.

Turning to face Olivia, Meredith said, "I'm here to help Kev. I know you are confused and suspicious of me showing up like this. Please let me explain, then you will understand." Nodding, Olivia sat down, feeling nervous of the unknown. Meredith remained standing, took a deep breath, and began.

"My parents divorced when I was young. I divided my time living with the both of them for many years. It wasn't bad, as they remained friends, so it was easier for me. Better than most kids have it. When I was in my last year of high school, my father met Victoria Price."

Stunned, Olivia sat up straighter, her mouth dropping open. Meredith held her hand up. "Don't say anything. Let me keep going. Talking about my father is very difficult for me. He was the kindest, gentlest man I have ever known. He worked hard as an accountant and built a very successful business. He was very wealthy and was always attracting the wrong kind of woman. He was average-looking and knew he had to be careful of women who wanted a rich husband." Meredith clenched her hands. "That's until he met Victoria. He let his guard down and fell right into her spell. She could be so charming, and of course she was very beautiful. He fell for her like a fool. He was so blinded by her charms that he couldn't see her for who she really was. I saw right through her and knew what an evil soul she possessed.

"I can't explain how I know, I just do. I have always had a sixth sense about people. I guess that's why I'm so good at being an investigative journalist. After they were married I spent less time with my father and moved in full time with my mother. I couldn't stand to stay at their house. Frankly, that woman gave me the chills and scared me to death. The times Dad wasn't around she would look at me with cold, black eyes. She told me once to give up, my father was all hers now and he didn't have time for a little whore like me. I stopped going to the house and would meet Dad at different places. I pleaded with him to see her for who she really was. He didn't believe me and would become upset, telling me I was jealous, that I needed to grow up, I wasn't a little girl anymore. In the end I never mentioned her again when we were together."

Tears sprang to her eyes as she softly said, "They were married just over five years when he died." Pausing, she inhaled deeply. "When he was murdered—"

Olivia stood up, "By Victoria."

Nodding, Meredith replied, "Yes, how did you know?"

"Because she has murdered before."

"I don't believe this." Turning away from Olivia, Meredith took several quick breaths, hyperventilating. "Oh my god, she's killed before she met my dad? I knew she was evil. It's my fault. I should have convinced him of how horrible she really was. I could have prevented his death."

Grabbing her by the arm and turning her around to face her, Olivia said, "No, his death was not your fault. How could you have known? I didn't even know what she was capable of until this week. She is an actress that leads people to believe what she wants them to. Meredith, please go on and tell me what happened."

Inhaling deeply to slow her breathing, she continued, "Dad had a heart condition." She shook her hand in front of her chest. "An irregular heart rhythm."

Nodding Olivia clarified, “Atrial fibrillation.”

“Yes, that’s it. He was prescribed Warfarin to prevent blood clots. He was very diligent about taking his medicine correctly and getting his blood tested to make sure it was not too thick or thin. That’s why it came as such a horrible shock that when he died, they told me his blood was too thin. The blood test’s INR was dangerously high. Apparently he had gone out to the garage and tripped over a box that had been left on the bottom step. He fell onto the concrete, striking his head. The doctors told me the impact caused his brain to bleed.

“Intracranial hemorrhage,” Olivia whispered.

Nodding, Meredith said, “Yes, it was a massive bleed that caused his brain to swell. He died soon after arriving at the hospital.” Tears fell down her cheeks. “I loved him so much. My heart aches for him every day. I miss him, Olivia.”

With tears in her own eyes, Olivia replied, “I know, I know.”

Wiping her tears away, Meredith continued, “After the shock had eased some, I started thinking. How could his level have been that high? Why was a box left on the step? When did he get his last INR checked? I had to find out the answers. I couldn’t believe that this was a freak accident. I knew my dad too well. He was too meticulous to allow his INR to become too high. He wouldn’t have left a box on the step; he was way too organized. I had a horrific feeling that Victoria had something to do with it. She gained all his wealth with his death.

“I began asking questions. Kev told me that his mother organized my father’s medications because she didn’t want him to mix them up. He was older than she was, but not forgetful. He was very sharp. I asked a few of his close friends how he had been getting along with Victoria. Several of them confirmed that they were having problems.

"His best friend told me Dad wanted to divorce her; he suspected she may have been having an affair. In my gut I knew she had killed him, I just had to find out how. I went to Dad's home when she wasn't there. I searched his study and found the past year's receipts from the anticoagulation clinic where he had his INR checked. The level of his blood and the dosage he was to take was listed on the receipt after each visit. I could not find the receipts for the last two weeks of his life. I called the clinic identifying myself as his doctor's nurse. It was easier back then to gain information, not like today with the strict privacy laws. They told me he had not been in for an INR for two weeks prior to his death. It was noted his wife had cancelled his appointments, telling them they were going on vacation. He was going to have his INR checked at the resort's medical clinic.

"Kev told me where they had vacationed and I contacted the resort. They didn't have a medical clinic that checked lab work. I called the area's medical clinics and they did not have a record of him being there. I went back to Dad's home and looked everywhere for the Warfarin bottles. They were gone and so were the coagulation clinic receipts. I had no proof to how many pills were missing or when the medication was last filled. I attempted to convince a detective, but it was futile. I didn't have any evidence, only suspicion. I was helpless. I tried to enlist Kev's help, but he became furious with me. He couldn't understand how I could accuse his own mother of murder. I was helpless. I left the country weeks after his death. I've thrown myself into my work and have not looked back."

"Meredith, why are you here now? How does this relate to Kev?"

"Don't you see that she's poisoning Kev, her own son?"

"No, he has leukemia. He has battled it on and off for years."

"Does he, Olivia?" Olivia had a bewildered look on her face as she stared dumbfounded at Meredith. "Think about it, Olivia, look how Kev is normally strong, healthy, and fit. He has become sick on three occasions at random times. It doesn't make any sense. Wouldn't a person with chronic leukemia be sickly most of the time?"

"How do you know this?"

"Even though Kev and I don't stay in touch, I keep up to date on how he is through an old friend of ours. Kev and I may have left it on a bad note, but that didn't mean I stopped caring about him. I thought one day maybe we would be able to make amends. My friend and I both know Victoria is an evil and unbalanced woman. She will do anything to have her own way. She keeps a tight-fisted control on Kev's life and she had succeeded in controlling him up until he found you."

"But it doesn't make sense. Why make him sick? And how on earth would she be able to give him leukemia? This is crazy."

"I've done some very extensive research. Certain drugs can mimic leukemia. Not give you leukemia, but give you the symptoms of leukemia."

"My head is swimming in possibilities. I seriously don't know what to believe. One thing I do know: I wouldn't put it past her sick mind to do something as horrible and twisted as this. Meredith, would you come home with me and talk to Kev's dad and my cousin about your theory? We need to put our heads together and figure this out."

"Of course."

"Thank you. I need to make some phone calls first. Can you come home with me?"

"Yes, I'll follow you home."

CHAPTER 27

Jimmy and Kerri could hear the loud screech of tires from where they were sitting on the deck. The slamming of a car door, followed by the loud bang as the kitchen door hit the wall, quickly got their attention. They both ran into the house just as Olivia flew into the kitchen followed by a tall blonde woman. "Whoa, slow down, looks like something is chasin' you."

"Oh Jimmy," she cried as she ran into his arms.

"Struth. You're shakin' like a leaf."

"What's going on, Olivia?" Kerri asked, alarmed. Stepping back, Olivia attempted to explain but struggled to get a coherent word out.

Walking up to Jimmy and Kerri, Meredith introduced herself, "I'm Meredith Stevens, Kev's former stepsister. Can we sit and I'll explain everything?"

"Yeah, we can go out to the deck. Kerri and I were just havin' a cuppa. I'll make you both one."

"Olivia is going to need something stronger than that. Bring her a few fingers of whiskey," Kerri said as she ushered Olivia and Meredith out to the deck. Jimmy joined them with two hot coffees and a shot of whiskey for Olivia. Handing her the glass, Jimmy told her "Here, love, this will settle your nerves. Go on and throw it back."

Her hand was shaking as she put the glass to her lips, tilted her head back, and swallowed the lot. Coughing and making a face, Olivia squeaked out, "Shit. I don't drink whiskey, and now I remember why."

"Good on ya, love, now take a sec and tell us what's goin' on."

Meredith spoke first. She recited what she had told Olivia a half hour ago. She barely made it to the end, as Jimmy and Kerri were raving mad and kept interrupting. Jimmy got up from the table and started to pace. "How in the world could she do something like this? Kill her husband and that other bloke. I knew she didn't have a heart, but to do this to her own son? Her own flesh and blood? I can't wrap my head around it," he said, shaking his head.

Kerri said vehemently, "She's a heartless, psycho bitch."

By this time Olivia had calmed and started to think logically. Putting her hands up, she told them, "We have to think. If this is really not leukemia, then what poison could mimic leukemia?"

"Never heard of such a thing," Jimmy replied.

"Could it be possible?" Kerri asked.

Removing a notebook from her bag, Meredith explained, "I've done some research on this. When I heard from my mother and friend that Kev had leukemia, then went into remission, I didn't think anything of it. But when I found out he was married and relapsed again, I became suspicious. So I did some digging around. I've talked to some experts and found there are drugs and chemicals that can cause leukemia. Leukemia is a cancer, and the only way to diagnose it is to do a biopsy. In the case of blood cancers, a bone biopsy would be done."

"So you think she is poisoning him? But how could the doctors think he has leukemia? They would have done the biopsy like you said," Kerri asked, perplexed.

"My suspicion is that she has falsified his medical records. I have more investigation to do to prove it. What we need first is to find out what chemical or drug she is using and how she is administering it."

The realization that Kev could really be poisoned hit them like a hammer, momentarily rendering them all speechless. Olivia stood and gathered the coffee mugs, "Come on, we have to go to David's house right now!"

"Who's David?" Meredith asked.

"Dr. David O'Day, a very good friend and the director of the Palliative Care program. He used to have a practice in hematology and oncology. He can help us figure out what chemical she could be using."

They arrived at David's home within five minutes of leaving the house, with Kerri driving. David answered the persistent banging on his door with irritation. As he opened the door, Olivia brushed past him, talking fast, "David, I'm sorry for barging in like this, but I need your help."

David stepped back, allowing Jimmy, Kerri, and Meredith to enter the foyer. Concern replaced his feelings of irritation. "Olivia, what is it? Is it Kev?"

"We believe he is being poisoned," she cried.

"Olivia, Kev has leukemia, you know that."

Olivia quickly interrupted him, "No, you have to listen to us. Just give us some time and we will explain everything." Skeptical, David suggested they follow him to the study. He led them into a large, tastefully-decorated room lined with books and artwork. A beautiful antique mahogany desk was centered near the windows. Olivia introduced Meredith to David. Kerri noticed that Meredith's good looks didn't get past him. Smiling to herself, she propped herself on the windowsill, as Olivia and Meredith sat in front of the desk, each in cushioned wooden chairs. Jimmy paced in the shadows. Meredith once again recited her earlier conversation with Olivia, explaining the death of her father, answering David's questions, and going into more detail when asked. Knowing he was not fully convinced, she asked that he look at some of the research she had done.

"Dr. O'Day," Meredith started.

"No, call me David."

"Alright," she said, smiling. "David. Let's pretend this is a case study in medical school. Remove Kev from the scenario and only focus on the plausibility of inducing an illness with a chemical or drug."

"I can keep an open mind."

Meredith removed her notebook, passing it to David. As he glanced through her notes, she explained, "I have researched chemicals, plants, prescription medications, and historical drugs used to murder people. The popular drugs like cyanide, arsenic, belladonna, and hemlock. These are highly fatal drugs that induce death quite quickly. So of course they were eliminated from my list."

Standing, she walked over and stood behind David and leaned over his shoulder. She flipped the pages of her notebook toward the back and pointed with her finger as she explained, "I had to find something that could be given that would cause an illness and not death. After an extensive search, I came across a drug used in the treatment of organ transplants. It's a medication that prevents the rejection of a kidney transplant by weakening the body's immune system to prevent the body from rejecting the new organ."

David interrupted, "Kev didn't have a transplant. How would Victoria gain access to a drug like this?"

"It's also used in the treatment of severe rheumatoid arthritis, Crohn's disease, or ulcerative colitis, usually when other drugs have failed."

"Azathioprine!" David muttered aloud, deep in thought. Turning to face Meredith, he stated, "I think you may be onto something. This drug can certainly give a person the side effects of leukemia. But none of this makes sense. You have to have a biopsy to receive a diagnosis of leukemia, and how would she get a prescription for this? I don't believe his mother has rheumatoid arthritis."

"She is obtaining the drug from a physician who thinks she has R.A."

"How do you know that?"

"Because she lived with my dad, and I lived there too. I have seen a prescription for it before. I once picked up several prescriptions for my dad, and I remember she became so angry with me because I had picked them up that day. It wasn't something I usually did. Dad thought since I was in the area it was easier for me than having Victoria go out."

"Why would a physician even prescribe this drug to her? I've met her; she obviously does not have R.A."

"I swear she has falsified her medical records. I've seen it done before in other cases I've worked."

"Now that would be incredible. Do you have any idea how difficult that would be to do?"

"Today, yes, but ten years ago it would have been easier. The privacy laws and access to records were way more lax back then."

Jimmy, Olivia, and Kerri broke the silence by filling the room with questions.

"How much would she be givin' him?"

"How would you administer it?"

"Where would the bitch hide it?"

Standing up, David held his arms up, talking above them, "One at a time."

Olivia walked to the window, deep in thought as the others continued to pepper him with questions. After several minutes, she abruptly turned to them and said, "We have to go to Victoria's home now. We have to find proof, and the only way is by finding the Azathioprine. We need hard evidence." Olivia looked directly at Meredith, thinking of her father's death. She returned the look with a grim smile and nodded.

"Kerri, I need you to go to the hospital and keep an eye on Victoria. In an hour it will be her visiting time. Don't let her leave until you have the clear from me. Jimmy and Meredith, you come with me. We will need all the hands we can get to search her place. David, you better stay here; the less involved the better."

"No, I can help."

"You would be helping more if you could do some more research on the Azathioprine. The more we know, the greater chances we have of treating it for Kev's recovery."

"Yes, you are right. Call me if you find anything."

"Thanks, David," Olivia said as she gave him a quick hug. "Come on, let's go," she yelled out as she rushed for the door.

They had arrived over an hour ago, accessing the house by the back door using Kev's set of keys. Meeting back in the kitchen, they looked defeated. They had searched every possible place in the house twice. "It's got to be here," Jimmy sighed, frustration lacing his voice. "Why would she hide the medicine when she probably has a prescription for it?"

Olivia answered her ringing phone. "Any luck, Liv?"

"No, we've looked everywhere."

"Heads up. You don't have much time. The nurse told me that Victoria said she was going to be leavin' soon."

"You have to keep her there. We need more time, Kerri."

"I don't know how to stall. She knows I hate her friggin' guts, so I can't just go in there and have a chat."

Panicking, Olivia said, "Oh shit, we have to find this."

"I s'pose I could go flatten her tires."

"Mmm, no, I've got it. Tell Suzanna to switch Kev's screen to teaching mode. Have her put it on an arrhythmia so it looks like he's not doing well."

"What?"

"Just tell her what I told you. She'll know what I mean."

"Won't she get in trouble?"

"No, she'll do it." Olivia quickly disconnected and turned back to Meredith and Jimmy. "Okay, that might buy us a little more time. Jimmy, you knew Victoria better than we do. Where would she hide something she wouldn't want found?"

"Struth, that was a long time ago, I never knew anything she hid, at least that I found."

"Think!" The women yelled in unison. Jimmy walked out of the kitchen as Meredith opened the freezer to search again. Olivia watched Jimmy as he bent down to the fireplace. He moved his hand under the grate, around the walls and into the chimney. Nothing. Disappointed, Olivia began to turn away when suddenly Jimmy yelled out "No! She wouldn't have. Would she?"

Puzzled, Olivia and Meredith looked at Jimmy as he jumped up and ran to the garage. They followed and found Jimmy scanning the garage, then setting his sights on a large toolbox standing in the corner near the back door. He strode over to it and shoved it away from the wall. He dropped to his knees and began running his fingers around a line in the concrete.

"Liv, hand me that screwdriver, right there on the wall," he commanded. Olivia quickly handed it to him. She missed it at first, but as she watched Jimmy pry the tip on the screwdriver under a straight line in the concrete, she realized there was a rectangular outline that was about twelve by ten inches and a shade darker than the rest of the concrete. The women watched in amazement as Jimmy popped off the top of the concrete, revealing a hole. He reached in and pulled out a medication bottle that read 'Azathioprine.' "Cripes," Jimmy whispered under his breath as Meredith and Olivia gasped.

Olivia whispered, "Oh my god, Jimmy, just like the axe."

His voice flat he replied, "Yeah, the irony of it, Olivia."

CHAPTER 28

Before leaving Victoria's, they had agreed to meet at Olivia's home the next morning around 8:00 a.m. They had placed the bottle of Azathioprine back in the hiding place. They didn't want her to know they were on to her. No telling what she would do. Olivia and Kerri were making coffee while Jimmy left earlier to get some pastries. He had said he needed some time alone to clear his head and sort all this buggery out. He had walked to the bakery, turning down Kerri's offer to drive him. Kerri asked Olivia "What do you think of everything that has happened the past twenty-something hours?"

"I haven't given myself time for this to completely sink in, but if I did I don't think I would be able to function. To be honest, this is scaring the hell out of me. I feel like I'm trapped in a murder mystery horror movie. This does not seem real."

"It shouldn't be real. This is really whacked," Kerri responded as there was a knock on the door, "I'll get it."

As she walked out of the kitchen, Jimmy came in through the back sliding glass door with a large bag of pastries. "Did the walk do you any good?"

"Yeah, I reckon so, had a good old think."

"Come to any conclusions?"

"Yeah, I should've left her years ago, before anything like this could happen. I should've listened back then when everyone told me she wasn't right for me. Could've saved a lot of heartache if I had."

"Our lives certainly would have turned out different, but you can't blame yourself. How could you have known?"

Olivia turned to greet David and Meredith as they walked into the kitchen. "Look who I found, turned up at the same time." Kerri winked at Olivia behind their backs.

As greetings were exchanged there was another knock at the door, "Who could that be?" Jimmy asked

"I invited Suzanna over, Kev's nurse. We need her help. Plus she's one of my closest friends. She'll want in on whatever we decide to do. I'll meet you in the dining room." Olivia opened the door, "Hi," they said in unison as they exchanged a warm hug.

"When I got your cryptic message, I knew I had to be here. Something isn't right, I can sense it. What's going on?"

"You'll find out soon enough. Come in with a clear mind and form your own opinion. You are going to hear some very crazy stories that are horrifically true."

"Don't be so sure I'd be that surprised. Oh, Oliva, Victoria knows Jimmy is here."

"What! How?" Olivia asked shocked

"One of the nurses casually said to Victoria how happy she must be that Kev's dad is here."

"Oh shit, what will she do now?"

"I don't know, but let's not worry too much just yet. Come on, let's go in and see everyone."

Everyone was already seated around the table. Olivia did quick introductions for Suzanna and Meredith. The group was equipped with coffee, pastries and notepads. Olivia began, "Thank you for all being here. It means a lot to Kev and me." All at the table nodded in acknowledgement, each thinking they would rather be nowhere else but here for them. "Let's go over everything we know so far. Each of us have some type of information about Victoria. If we piece what we know all together, we may be able to find out what she is up to and her eventual plan."

"Her plan is to kill her own son," Kerri stated matter-of-factly.

Olivia saw a flicker of horror and fear on each person's face as they acknowledged the reality of the truth.

"What do you mean, trying to kill him?" Suzanna asked, shocked.

"That's what we are going to figure out," Olivia answered. "Jimmy, you were married to her, you were there for the first murder she committed." Suzanna inhaled sharply. The group glanced at her, nodding. Olivia continued "Kerri, you knew her when you were a child and spoke to Kev's grandmother. Suzanna, you have been Kev's nurse each time he was ill. You have seen Victoria's behavior when she visits. Meredith, you knew her when she was married to your father and her involvement in his death. David, you have met her also and you have medical knowledge of cancer. Let's start with what we know. Jimmy, Victoria had an affair while you were married. Do you know how serious it was? Was she going to leave you for him?"

"I dunno, Liv. I heard rumors of the affair, and yeah, I knew she'd leave me at some point, but reckoned it wouldn't have been with that bloke."

"Why not?"

"Cause he had a lot goin' for him. He was married to the daughter of a very wealthy lawyer. He didn't come from money; he needed hers and her daddy's power."

Interrupting, Meredith asked, "Do you have a whiteboard or chalkboard so we could write down an outline of the important events?"

"I have a large poster board," Olivia replied.

"Thank you, and a marker too, please."

Olivia returned with the poster board and taped it to the dining room wall. Seated again, she continued, "Jimmy, why do you think she murdered that man?"

Those who didn't know the details were stunned, but did not comment. "Umm, at the time she said he was pushing her around, he was gonna hurt her. I didn't believe it. He wasn't the type. He struck me as a wussie. I'd bet on it that he broke it off with her. She doesn't take well to any type of rejection." Meredith stood up and wrote on the poster, "Murder of lover."

Olivia turned to Suzanna. "You have known Kev longer than any of us as an adult. You have cared for him each time he was sick. What stands out in your mind?"

"I thought it was odd that Kev looked so strong and healthy, and he didn't look like someone that was suffering from an illness. The first time he became sick he had just graduated from college. He had a job offer in Boston. The second time, his company wanted to transfer him to England, it was a really good opportunity. Then he was making plans to launch his company in Australia. That's when you found each other. Now here he is, sick again."

Kerri and Olivia said in unison, "Moving to Australia, back to Hay."

Olivia took in a large gulp of air, "Oh no, because we were leaving!"

Meredith jotted down:

Kev

Leaving for a job

Leaving for a job transfer

Leaving for Australia

Jimmy sighed, "She couldn't live without him."

"But why kill him now?" Kerri asked confused.

Olivia interrupted, "Let's keep going. Meredith, she was married to and killed your father. We can't prove it, but let's go on the premise she did."

"I have talked to some old employees of my dad's since I've been back. Several have verified that Dad and Victoria were having some problems. There were rumors that he wanted a divorce. With the information we have now, I'm certain he wanted to leave her. It's the only thing that makes sense on why she would murder him."

With fire in her eyes, Meredith wrote, "Murdered my father." They all studied the four points, each one thinking of a reason why. *Murdering a lover, husband, and now a son.*

"Black widow," Kerri mumbled.

David frowned and asked, "What about her childhood, her parents?"

"When I visited your mum, Jimmy, right before I found you, she mentioned what an unbalanced woman Victoria was. Said it was a surprise because she was a sweet little girl before her dad left," Kerri said.

Straightening in his chair, Jimmy exclaimed, "That's right, she hated her mother. She always blamed her for her dad leaving."

David said what they were all thinking. "She felt abandoned."

They sat in silence as they absorbed this information. Meredith wrote "father left" at the top of the list. David waited for a response; when none came, he explained, "Abandonment represents fear felt to the very core. It festers into a wound that contains all the losses felt, even all the way back to childhood. It's like grief over a loss of a loved one, but the person hasn't died. They have just chosen not to be with you. People lose their self-esteem and feel a strong sense of loneliness and a loss of self-worth."

"But people don't kill because of it," stated Suzanna.

"No, they normally don't," David replied. "They find ways of coping, either through time, therapy, new relationships, or in severe cases drugs, alcohol, or inappropriate behaviors. In this case, Victoria probably has an undiagnosed mental illness that has been exacerbated by the rejection she has felt each time someone she cared about wanted to leave her. She felt a strong sense of abandonment. I think the first murder resulted from the severe loss she felt over losing her father. I'm speculating she was very close to him. She couldn't resolve the intense feelings of abandonment. So when her lover rejected her, all those unresolved emotions manifested into extreme rage. The only way she could cope was to take control. By killing him, he couldn't leave her. In her mind it probably gave her a sense of being in charge."

"Well, I don't feel sorry for her," Kerri challenged.

David held his hands up. "I know. I'm just trying to explain her mindset, so we know what we are dealing with and how best to handle her."

"We need to stay ahead of her next move," Suzanna stated.

Meredith replied, "Yes, we now know what she's doing and we think we know why. Now we need to stop her. And this time have hard evidence to put her away."

Everyone nodded in agreement.

Jimmy asked, "But how?"

Olivia answered, "We know that it's not likely Kev has leukemia, she had been poisoning him with the Azathioprine. We need to know how and when."

"What do you mean, poison?" Suzanna asked surprised.

They filled her in on what they had found at Victoria's and their strong suspicion that Kev didn't have leukemia. "That can't be possible, a drug can't mimic leukemia. It's a cancer. It's diagnosed with a biopsy."

"Yes, we realize that. What we need to find out next is whether a biopsy was done here at Harbor Lake," Olivia said.

Meredith explained, "When Kev was finishing his last year at Westwood University, Victoria moved there to be near him. She worked for a short time as a coding specialist at a hospital. I believe she had falsified someone else's medical records who had leukemia. She had access to hundreds of patients' charts."

Shocked, Suzanna exclaimed, "That's premeditation. How could she have planned to do this?"

David answered, "She knew Kev would be graduating and would soon be looking for a job, most likely away from her. She couldn't allow him to leave her. This was her way of controlling him."

Suzanna suddenly stood up and shook her hands in the air, clearly upset, "But this time, she really is killing him. He was improving until she found out Jimmy had been found and was coming to see him. This is insane."

Everyone turned to her in surprise. Seeing the question on their faces, Suzanna explained how Victoria knew that Jimmy was here.

Meredith said in agreement, "Yes, I think her initial reasoning was to just make him sick for a while to prevent Kev from moving to Australia with Olivia. Now that Jimmy is here, he is a huge threat. Kev will want to know what happened back then. He will find out that she murdered a man and pinned it on his father. He may not want a relationship with her once he finds out what she has done. She is at risk of him leaving her."

Kerri summed it up, "If she can't have him, then no one can."

David agreed, "Yes, her last act of control."

"Then how do we stop her?" Jimmy asked

"Tell me more about the drug," Suzanna asked.

David explained, "It's a medication used for severe rheumatoid arthritis. If ingested it can cause anemia, fatigue, and abnormal blood cell counts. In large doses it can be fatal, but in smaller, less concentrated doses with slower ingestion time, the symptoms can be less severe."

Understanding, Suzanna summarized, "The symptoms are similar to leukemia, so the treatment plan would be the same. It knocks his white cell count down, leaving him susceptible to infections. When this happens, we are treating the infection in his body. He has had pneumonia and bacteremia, a bloodstream infection. So what we end up doing is treating the infection, not specifically the leukemia."

"Yes, that's right," David agreed.

Meredith asked, "Then how is she administering it and when?"

Kerri replied, "Well, we know just like last night she comes between five and seven o'clock, right Suzanna?"

"Yes, she does," Suzanna slowly agreed, lost in thought.

"But how's she givin' it to him, when he is out of it and can't swallow with that bloody tube shoved down his throat?" Jimmy questioned.

"It can't be IV," Olivia stated as she looked over at David for confirmation.

"No Azathioprine would be very corrosive if injected into a vein. It would burn the tissue, resulting in a very severe phlebitis."

"It's his feeding tube!" Suzanna exclaimed.

Everyone turned to look at her as she sat forward in excitement, "His feeding tube equipment. It's changed at 6:00 p.m. every evening. I always organize my care ahead of time and lay things out in the room in anticipation of when I need to use them. I have the feeding bag and two cans of formula at the bedside. At 6:00 p.m. I take the old bag down, flush his feeding tube, fill the new bag with formula, and connect it."

Coming to the same conclusion, Olivia and Kerri said, "She puts the Azathioprine in the new feeding bag."

"That's very plausible. It's a full 480 ml of formula, enough volume to administer in a less concentrated dose," David explained.

Suzanna interrupted, "She has to be doing it this way. I noticed last week when she wasn't visiting two days in a row."

"There was an improvement in his blood counts," Suzanna and Olivia yelled out simultaneously.

As the realization sank in that a person they all cared very much about was slowly being murdered, a feeling of fear shrouded the room. As David looked at each person seated around the table, he knew they were all experiencing a sense of shock. He has seen this reaction in many patients he had given bad news to. Taking charge, he got up from the chair and spoke, "This is enough for today. I think everyone is feeling a sense of shock, and you need time to think and come to terms with the implications. I will confer with Dr. Breland, Kev's oncologist. I also need to find Kev's original medical records to determine if they were really falsified with a diagnosis of leukemia. I need to see if there was a biopsy done. We have to obtain all the evidence we can to prove this. We can't go to the authorities without it. I'm also ordering a test to check for the byproduct of the Azathioprine. Suzanna, on your shifts you must act like you have before. We can't arouse her suspicions. Also, you need to dispose of the tube feeding after Victoria has left and put new formula up that has not been tampered with. Meredith, I need you to contact the hospital Victoria worked at. See if they have any medical records on Kev. Olivia can sign a medical release for his records so they can be faxed to us. Let's meet in two days. That should be enough time to get the lab results back and locate his original medical records."

As everyone stood up to leave, Jimmy said, "Hang on a tick. If Kev doesn't get the poison, won't he start gettin' better?"

"Yeah, you're right," Kerri agreed.

Everyone turned to David for an answer, "He will improve slowly, not too quickly that she will notice. We will see improvements in his blood counts."

"What if he starts waking up?" Meredith asked.

Suzanna answered, "We could keep him lightly sedated for a few days."

"I don't want it to be for long. He has suffered enough. We need to move fast and smart, to have her caught and arrested," Olivia demanded. "I won't allow this to go on much longer." They understood and didn't take offense to her anger, because they felt exactly the same way.

CHAPTER 29

"I'm sorry I ran out the other day and had you fill in for me on the Harrison family," Olivia apologized.

"Oh, that's okay, I understand. I knew the case, so I didn't mind helping," Rose replied.

"Well, I appreciated it. How did it go?"

"It went as good as expected for a family that faced such a difficult decision. The family didn't want Mr. Harrison to suffer. It was important to them to respect his wishes."

"I'm so glad for Mr. Harrison. They gave him his last gift. To follow his wishes and allow him to die," Olivia said sadly.

"Is everything alright? You seem more distracted than usual the past couple of days."

"No, no, I'm good. You know, I'm just worried about Kev. I just want him to recover."

"Oh yeah, how is he doing?"

"About the same, he is slowly improving. Well, I must run. I've got a million things to do. Thanks again for your help," she replied as she hung up the phone.

"Ahh," Olivia groaned, leaning back in her chair as she looked up at the ceiling. She experienced a sudden onset of dizziness and an overwhelming sense of nausea. She lurched forward, reached for the garbage bin, and vomited. Coughing and catching her breath, she reached for a tissue to wipe her watery eyes and dry the spit from her mouth. *That was weird,* she thought, *I don't usually have a nervous stomach, but then again I've never been involved in murder before.* She took a gulp of water and tied the garbage bin liner.

Leaving the office, she walked into the ICU, opened the dirty utility room door, and threw the bag into the dumpster. Exiting the room, she walked around the nurses' station, saying good morning to various staff as they were going about their work. Pushing Room 7's door open, she said, "Morning, Suzanna."

"Hi Olivia, how are you?"

She walked closer to Suzanna, lowering her voice. "I'm a bundle of nerves. How about you? Are you holding up?"

"I'm doing better than I thought I would around her. I really deserve an Academy Award."

Laughing, Olivia replied, "If we get her, you'll get your award when this is over." She walked over to Kev. He looked comfortable and still so handsome. She felt an overwhelming sense of love—her heart felt tight. She noticed the vent settings and Kev's breathing. Turning quickly to Suzanna, she excitedly whispered, "Suzanna! He is off SIMV, breathing on his own."

"Yes, I couldn't wait to tell you. When I got here this morning the night shift had weaned him off the vent doing all the work for him. It's supporting his own breathing with a little spurt of pressure to help him take deeper breaths." Exhaling a huge sigh of relief, Olivia kissed Kev on the cheek. Taking his hand, she squeezed tightly and told him he was going to be alright. Smiling at Suzanna, she asked, "How are his labs this morning?"

"If Victoria asks, they are the same. If you ask me, his counts are almost normal. He is no longer neutropenic or anemic. His white count is normal, he has been afebrile for over forty-eight hours, his secretions are drying up, and the infiltrate on his chest X-ray has almost resolved. I'd say that when he is off the sedation he will wake up. I did a sedation holiday for a few hours earlier and he followed commands. I had to re-sedate him, as he was getting a bit agitated from the ET tube."

Holding her hands to her chest, Olivia said a silent prayer that all would go well in the next thirty-six hours. "You'll be at my house this evening for our meeting?"

"Of course I'll be there, I'm anxious to see what information they have found. I want the plan so we can get this over with to get Kev home to you."

Olivia gave Suzanna a reassuring hug. "Thanks for everything; you are a good friend and nurse. I don't think Kev would ever have survived without you."

"Oh, come on, it wasn't just me. Everyone here did a great job. Now go on, I'm busy saving lives here," Suzanna said, a little embarrassed from the praise.

Olivia gave Kev another kiss and whispered, "I love you." For the first time in a long time, she felt hope. Smiling, she walked out of the door. "I'll see you tonight."

CHAPTER 30

Meredith and David were sitting in the living room looking over Kev's medical records. Jimmy was on the deck watching the sun go down over the water. He was quiet after arriving home from visiting Kev at the hospital. Olivia stood at the sink washing the dishes. As Kerri picked up another plate to dry, she asked, "You alright, Liv? You hardly touched your tea tonight."

"I'm alright, I'm just so nauseous. This whole thing is getting to me. I want Kev home and for us to return to the normal life we had."

"Hang in there a little longer, it's almost over."

"I wish Suzanna would hurry up and get here."

"She should be here any minute. Her shift was up a little while ago."

Hearing a knock on the door, Kerri said, "Speak of the devil."

Olivia walked out to the deck to get Jimmy. He was facing the lake with his arms on the railing. Placing her hand on his shoulder, she asked, "Are you alright?"

Clearing his throat, his voice caught as he said, "Yeah, just thinkin' bout things. A lot of time has gone by. I always believed I would see Kev again, I never lost hope. Just now, seein' him at the hospital, I can't get over that it's actually him." He swallowed to hold back the tears that were threatening to fall. "I s'pose I'm a little scared, Liv. What's he goin' to think 'bout me after all these years? Is he gonna remember how much I loved him?"

Laying her head on his arm with her arm around his shoulders, Olivia replied, "He does love you, and he always has, even when he thought you were dead."

Smiling sadly, he said, "I wish I could turn back time and never have answered the phone that night. Look at the years we were robbed of."

"I feel the same way. We can't ever get those years back. What we can do is look forward. We get through tonight and the future is ours. We are taking our lives back. Now come on in so we can figure out how to do this."

"Righto. Ahh, Liv, thanks for finding me. At the time you didn't know I was innocent, but you went looking for me anyway."

"Jimmy, I knew in my heart you weren't a murderer, and you know I would do anything for Kev."

"Thank God you did, thank God you did."

They walked in the house and found everyone seated once again around the dining room table. David was at the head of the table with a stack of folders. Placing his hand on the folders, he explained, "These are Kev's medical records from Harbor Lake. I have gone through each office visit and hospitalization thoroughly. Each time he was hospitalized he presented the exact same way, treated and responded the same in each case. After each recovery he was given a few short rounds of chemo, then went into remission. What I didn't find was a record of a bone marrow biopsy done here. Dr. Breland never did one, as his mother insisted it wasn't necessary. She didn't want to put him through that again and risk infection.

She provided a bone marrow biopsy that was done at another hospital."

"Shouldn't Dr. Breland have insisted repeating it?" Olivia asked.

"Yes, he told me he had tried on several occasions. He finally admitted that Victoria could be very charming and persuasive, and Kev went along with what his mother insisted on."

"Oh no, another fool falling for her bull," Kerri muttered under her breath.

Ignoring Kerri's remark, David continued, "It was a little harder tracking down the records that Victoria had given Dr. Breland from Grace General Hospital in Boston. I won't bore you with the details, just say there were a lot of files I went through in their storage rooms. I found the bone marrow biopsy, and it confirmed that Kev did have documented leukemia. Meredith and I compared the faxed medical records with the records Victoria had produced. The records appeared legitimate, but Meredith's gut instinct to continue to scour the records, which she did for hours, paid off. Her exceptional investigative skills discovered that the font used in both sets of records were different."

"The font?" they all asked, puzzled.

"Yes the type of font that was used to type the reports. Meredith and I compared the faxed records directly received from Grace General Hospital with the records Victoria provided. It was subtle and something not likely noticed unless you were looking for it. Grace Hospital uses Times New Roman font, and the font used on the falsified records is Arial.

"Crikey, how did you know to look for that?" Jimmy asked, impressed.

Meredith answered, "It's what I do. I investigate. I did some work for an attorney's firm and came across something similar to this. Only then it was a will that was falsified."

"Unbelievable! The crazy lengths she went to," Kerri said, shaking her head.

David picked up a second folder. "This is the faxed medical records from Grace Hospital. Most of it was consistent until we read the bone marrow biopsy, bone marrow pathology report, and the blood work results. The bone marrow biopsy procedure looks authentic at a casual glance. I'm sure it was a real case on a patient that underwent a bone marrow biopsy. Again, if you weren't looking for it, you wouldn't have noticed a discrepancy in the dosage of sedation the patient was given. He was administered double the dosage of sedation a 175-pound man would be given. The drug used was Propofol—it's used to sedate a patient during the procedure as it is very painful. The effects of the drug wear off quickly. The dosage calculated is based on the patient's weight of one milligram per kilogram. Kev was around 175 pounds, according to his records. Without boring you with the math, I've calculated he should have received 12 mg intravenously. It's documented here the patient was given a total of 25 mg. Based on the calculations, the patient would have had to have been over 225 pounds."

Allowing them a moment to absorb this, David observed their reactions. Jimmy sat shaking his head. Meredith reached for Olivia's hand to reassure her. Kerri smiled. "We've got the cunning bitch now," she said.

David, frowning, opened another folder. "This contains Kev's record of when he was in college and was hospitalized for appendicitis a month before the biopsy. A general blood work panel was ordered in the emergency room to determine what was causing his severe abdominal pain. In a diagnosis of acute appendicitis it is normal to have an elevation in the white blood cell count, which was documented. What I also noted was that the differential in his blood cells was completely normal."

"What does a differential mean?" asked Kerri.

"It measures the percentage of each type of white blood cell that a person has in their bloodstream. It also indicates if there are any abnormal or immature cells. I looked at his blood work four weeks after the surgery when he moved back here. The blood results that Victoria provided Dr. Breland revealed his white blood cells were immature and abnormal. According to these results, Kev was definitely in the acute stages of leukemia. Comparing to one month ago, it is unlikely that he could have developed leukemia so quickly. Dr. Breland would have known this if he had Kev's accurate medical record. Because he didn't, he had to base his treatment plan based on the falsified records."

"But wouldn't he have had new blood work drawn when he was being treated?" Suzanna asked.

"Yes, he did, but by then he had already been poisoned with the Azathioprine altering his blood cells, supporting the diagnosis of leukemia."

"Is this enough for probable cause?" Jimmy asked.

"Yes, I think we have enough circumstantial evidence here, along with the bottle of Azathioprine.

"What do we do now? We know she was and is poisoning him. I'm tired of sitting around talking about this. I want to have her arrested now," Olivia said.

"I know, and we will, Olivia. Meredith and I have already been to the police station and talked with a detective. He believes us, but it took a lot of time and explaining to convince him. Once we showed him the medical records and pointed out all the discrepancies, he agreed to help us."

"How? When? Why doesn't he go and arrest her right now?" Olivia cried out in frustration, banging her fists on the table.

"We have a plan in place. She will be arrested tomorrow," Meredith said.

CHAPTER 31

There was barely any room to move in Olivia's office. Seated at the desk was Detective Malone, his hair receding and traces of grey lining his temples. He looked to be around 6' 2" with a lean, athletic body. Dressed in jeans, boots, and a pale blue shirt, he didn't look like a detective. When he took off his jacket, the gun holstered to his side and the badge on his belt gave him away.

David and Meredith were standing behind him talking to him about technicalities of the recording monitor. Kerri and Olivia were sitting quietly, too nervous to make conversation. Earlier this morning, an undercover cop dressed as a maintenance man had installed a camera in Kev's room. The equipment in Olivia's office had been set up so they could watch and record the activities in the room. The system didn't have audio capability, which was not a concern.

Glancing at the clock for what seemed the hundredth time, Olivia said to Kerri, "Where is she? It's almost 5:30 p.m. Oh god, I hope she's not onto us."

"She'll be here, try to relax."

"I can't. I feel like I'm going to throw up again."

David quietly stated, "She's here."

Kerri and Olivia jumped up and stepped close to the screen. "Are you recording?" Olivia asked anxiously.

"Yes, started five minutes ago," replied Detective Malone.

They waited and watched as Suzanna adjusted Kev's sheets. Victoria seated herself next to Kev, her mouth moving, obviously talking to Suzanna.

"Look at that evil bitch," Kerri muttered under her breath. "Looking so concerned, it makes me sick." David glanced at her giving her a disapproving look. Kerri thought to herself that if he hadn't done so much for Kev, she'd tell him to remove that stick that's stuck up his bum.

Olivia nudged Kerri in the arm to get her attention. "Look, Suzanna is preparing the new tube feeding." They watched as Suzanna labeled the new bag. Victoria got up so Suzanna could reach the feeding tube pump. She disconnected the end from Kev's Dobhoff feeding tube that snaked down his nose and threw the old bag into the trash beside her. She efficiently hung the new bag, reconnected it to the Dobhoff, and set the pump to the correct settings. She said something to Victoria as she washed her hands, then left the room.

There was complete silence in the office as they waited. Squeezing Kerri's hand, Olivia held her breath as she saw Victoria reach into her purse. She stood up, looked over at the door, and took down the tube-feeding bag off the pole. Opening the cap of the bag, she quickly poured liquid from a small bottle into the formula.

Olivia heard the detective command into his handheld radio, "Move in now." Olivia felt an overwhelming sense of relief as she saw two uniformed policemen rush into the room with their weapons drawn.

Olivia and Kerri were the first to rush out of the office and into the unit. As they arrived in the doorway of Kev's room, they saw Victoria in handcuffs. "What are you doing?" Victoria demanded, "I'm visiting my ill son. Let go of me."

Detective Malone strode in and recited the Miranda rights as she kept on insisting that she had done nothing wrong. "What did you put in the feeding bag, ma'am? Trying to poison your son?" asked Detective Malone.

"What on earth are you talking about? Let me tell you—" Victoria said as Jimmy stepped around Olivia and Kerri and walked into the room. "Oh, Jimmy! Thank goodness it's you, I've missed you so much. Tell them I'd never hurt our boy, this is a mistake. They're accusing me of trying to poison Kev," she cried out.

"No, Vic. You're a selfish, cruel, miserable excuse for a mother. Our son didn't deserve everything you've put him through," he said, the anger searing off each word. "I hope you rot in that cell they're going to throw you in."

She began pulling against the officers restraining her, "You bastard, it's your fault. If you had been a better husband I'd never have looked for someone else to take care of me," she screamed.

"No! You have blood on your hands. It's all over now, the pain you have caused to so many people. You deserve to be locked up for the rest of your sorry life," he said as he turned and walked out of the room.

"You fucker, I should've killed you back then and not him!"

"And who would that have been, Mrs. Price?" Detective Malone asked.

She closed her mouth, calming herself. "I want to call my lawyer."

"Come on, let's go."

The officers, each holding one of her arms, followed behind the detective as they led her out of the room. As she passed Olivia, her cold black eyes bored into her. Menacingly, she said, "It should've been you lying in that bed. You're the one who took my son away." She laughed hysterically, "Well I've won, you can't have him, he'll be dead soon."

Olivia walked up to her and leaned in close, "No he won't. We found the Azathioprine you've been giving him. We figured out your twisted, sick game. He hasn't had any of that drug in days. He is actually going to be fine and will be with me for the rest of his life."

Olivia felt vindicated by seeing the shock and confusion on her face as the realization hit her. "You fucking bitch, I swear I'll kill you," she screamed hysterically as Kerri grabbed Olivia's arm and pulled her away.

Kerri smiled. "Enjoy prison, you sick bitch," and walked away with Olivia.

As the officers guided Victoria out of the ICU doors, Meredith was leaning against a wall. Victoria, enraged, yelled at her, "You! You little whore. You did this."

"Yes, for my dad," Meredith replied. "Now go to hell," she said as she turned and walked away.

EPILOGUE

The chiming of the doorbell interrupted Olivia's thoughts. She turned from the sink and reached for a hand towel. She hurriedly walked to the front door and opened it to find Meredith and David standing there with huge grins on their faces. "Meredith, David, I didn't expect you two," Olivia happily said as she reached to give them both a hug.

"When did you get back?"

"We flew in last night."

"Why didn't you tell me you were coming home?"

"We wanted to surprise you in person with our great news."

"What news? Tell me what happened. Are you moving back? Come in," Olivia said as she pulled them through the doorway.

"You haven't changed a bit, Olivia, with all of your questions," David laughed.

Meredith, holding David's hand, excitedly announced, "We got married."

Olivia jumped up with excitement. "Yes, I'm so happy for you both. Does this mean you'll finally be moving home?"

"Yes, we've been away almost three years now. It's time to settle down. I've been running away from life for so long now. With David's help, I'm coming to terms with the loss of my father. I need to take time and enjoy my mother and friends while I can. Olivia you have taught me the meaning of being with those you love, because you never know when they will be taken away. At the end of the day, the ones you love are the only thing in life that matters," Meredith explained.

Olivia smiled. "I know the ones we love give meaning to our life." Linking her arm through Meredith's and David's arms, she said, "Let's go down to the lake, I'll show you the meaning of mine."

They walked out of the house and down the walkway that led to the lake.

"Jimmy lives here now in a house not far from here, with his mother," said Olivia. "He brought her over and helps take care of her. She does really well for being in her eighties." Giggling, she lowered her voice. "And he is seeing a really nice lady friend."

"Never too late for love," Meredith laughed as she looked at David.

"Kerri's here too," Olivia said. David groaned.

"Oh come on, she's not that bad," Meredith chided him.

He rolled his eyes. "Well, she doesn't hold back on saying what's on her mind."

Ignoring him, Olivia said, "She's back and forth from Australia to here. She is doing really well selling her paintings to the American market. Oh, and Suzanna is stopping by later."

As they approached, everyone was seated in lawn chairs near the barbeque that Jimmy was tending to. They heard a child's squeal of delight. Then they saw a little boy with a head of pale blonde hair running toward them as fast as his little legs would carry him, his round little face full of excitement. "Mummy, Mummy, I catched a fishy all by myself," he yelled as he ran into Olivia's arms. She swept him up into the air and turned in a circle, "Oh, Kevin, that's wonderful, you're my little fisher boy."

Meredith laughed and patted him on the back. "Wow you're such a big boy, great job."

He unwrapped his arms from his mother's neck, held up three fingers, and said very seriously, "That's cause I'm free." Meredith and David laughed as Olivia bent down to put her squirming son back on his feet.

"I assume he was the cause of all your nausea and vomiting back then, Olivia?" David chided her.

"The best reason in the world to feel sick." Olivia smiled.

They watched him as he ran over to Jimmy. "Grandpa, Grandpa, can you help me put the worm on, and I'll show you how to catch a fishy?"

Jimmy, with pure adoration in his eye, said, "Of course, my little scallywag, you show me how."

Olivia led Meredith and David over to introduce them to Jimmy's mother and friend. As they talked, she turned away and looked to the far end of the dock. The light shone brilliantly on the water, giving it the illusion of twinkling stars. Blinking the light from her eyes, she saw his silhouette in the bright rays of fading sunlight. Her breath caught and her heart skipped several beats, as it often did when she would see him. At unexpected moments, her body would react in surprise as though her mind was telling her again: He is real, he is alive, and he is here with you.

Thinking back to when she almost lost him again sent a bolt of fear straight through her heart. She reminded herself that he was okay now, and Victoria was away for life, convicted of murder and attempted murder. She confessed to both murders, but adamantly denied the poisoning of Kev. She apparently had a mental breakdown, becoming catatonic. She was serving her time in a psychiatric prison. Kev didn't talk about her and was still working his way through the sad emotions that occasionally arose.

She slowly walked up to him, her smile and eyes reflecting the lifetime of love for him. Kev reached out and drew her against him, encircling his arms around her waist as she placed her arms around his neck. "I hear our son catched a fishy," Olivia said with happiness in her voice.

"He sure did, all on his own. Well, maybe just a little help from his dad."

Looking up at Kev, Olivia said, "He is so excited, he's now teaching Grandpa how to catch one too."

Kev bent down and kissed her tenderly, then a little more passionately. A soft moan escaped from Olivia's lips.

Kev lovingly breathed, "Oh, Funny Face."

They both said in unison, "I love you."

ACKNOWLEDGEMENTS

The writing of this book was a labor of love filled with imagination and the joy of memories that were woven into a fictional story. I have always had a love of books and a passion for the written word. Over the years I felt a story growing inside of me. It kept weaving throughout my mind until I realized I wanted to write a book.

I eventually voiced my dream to my husband, Jon Simcoke, who immediately supported and believed in me. He has always been by my side encouraging me and has had the utmost confidence that I would succeed. Many years ago, while visiting Australia, I told my sister, Erica Smith, of my dream to write a book. She went out and bought a purple notebook and a pen set. She gave them to me and told me to write my book. Their confidence in me was overwhelming. I am truly grateful to Jon and Erica for their encouragement. They helped me believe in myself.

That purple notebook holds the very first of my writing, and it's befitting that the final words to go into it now are the acknowledgments of my book. I want to give my heartfelt thanks to all those who have helped me over the years. To Jon for always loving and believing in me. To Erica Smith for getting me started. To my daughters, Alexandra-Maree Mesplay and Jessica Margaret Simcoke, who have always had pride and confidence in me. To my mother, Barbara Russell, who read some of my story and reminded me of my love for writing. To my father, Laurie Smith, who has been cheering me on over the years and giving me feedback. To my sister, Tara Hall, for reading my story, providing invaluable insights, and always supporting me. To my aunt, Kate Newton-Smith, who unknowingly inspired the title of the book. In her letters she would mention that the 'distance between us' seemed too far. To my favorite cousin, Kerri Weymouth, who inspired the creation of one of the characters. To my best friend, Susan Mudge, who helped me with one of the characters. To Robin Seaton-Jefferson for reading my early writing. She was my first editor and was so very encouraging. To Jenn Glick for reading my entire story. She gave me invaluable feedback that helped tie the story together. To my editor, Andrew Doty, and my book designer, Peggy Nehmen, whose professionalism and exceptional work made my book possible. They have guided me through the publishing world; without them I would still be navigating through the process. And to Tertia Butcher for reading my story and providing me with my first glowing review. She has become an incredible friend who helped me get the book to Australia, and I am grateful for all of her support.

With love and gratitude,

—Kyla

GLOSSARY

Australian words and sayings explained for American readers

Arvo: Afternoon
Akubra: Australian felt hat
Bloody block: Knock someone's head off
Bum: Buttocks
Cripes: Mild curse word
Crook: Sick
Fete: Carnival
Flash: Fancy
Footpath: Sidewalk
Get sacked: Fired
Hang on a tick: Wait a minute
Hooroo: Australian way of saying "goodbye"
Ks: Kilometers
Lollies: Candy
Miffed: Mad/angry
Op shop: Resale shop
Rouse: Yell at
Struth: An exclamation
Stubby: Short, glass bottle of beer
Tart: Promiscuous woman
Tea: Dinner
Tomato sauce: Ketchup
Whinging: Whining or complaining
Winfield Blues: Cigarettes
Yabby: Crawdad/crayfish

DEAR READER,

Thank you so much for reading *The Distance Between Us*. I hope you have enjoyed the story and found it compelling. I would love to hear your thoughts and ideas; please take a few minutes to post a review online. Even a few sentences would be greatly appreciated. I can be reached on Facebook at facebook.com/kylamareesimcoke (@kylamareesimcoke), and you can read more at read more at kylamareesimcoke.com.

—*Kyla*

Made in the USA
Lexington, KY
16 September 2018